THE QUICK HANGING

George Maledon, the Prince of Hangmen, just couldn't believe his eyes when he read that his old rival, Zeb Allen, had pulled off some cheap jackleg stunt involving a ten second drop. The Prince was determined to beat that time, on the death machine of his own invention. But persuading Judge Parker to come round to the unseemly notion of a speed hanging took every ounce of his guile — plus a strand of unexpected human weakness in the judge himself.

JEROME GARDNER

THE QUICK HANGING

Complete and Unabridged

LINFORD
Leicester

First published in Great Britain in 1991 by
Robert Hale Limited
London

First Linford Edition
published 1996
by arrangement with
Robert Hale Limited
London

British Library CIP Data

Gardner Jerome
    The quick hanging.—Large print ed.—
Linford western library
I. Title II. Series
823.914 [F]

ISBN 0–7089–7813–4   LP

Published by
F. A. Thorpe (Publishing) Ltd.
Anstey, Leicestershire

Set by Words & Graphics Ltd.
Anstey, Leicestershire
Printed and bound in Great Britain by
T. J. Press (Padstow) Ltd., Padstow, Cornwall

This book is printed on acid-free paper

1

GEORGE MALEDON had the usual few minutes to spare.

He allowed part of his attention to stray off among the crowd. Not that he was overly impressed by what he saw from his high vantage point. He could peg their number to a gnat's whisker after all these times. Three thousand wasn't much of a tribute to either the McCracken boys or to himself. And when his gaze wandered to the courthouse basement entrance, he could spy only a handful of bored looking reporters lolling on the iron rails. And all of them only local men at that.

It wasn't any more impressive either beyond the walls of the old stockade which had given Fort Smith its name. Times were when there'd been as many more packed outside the square as in it. Piled aboard horses and buckwagons and all manner of other rigs. And crawling all over the buildings theirselves. Hard to feature now that he'd seen them scrabbling with their unfeeling bloody hands at the glass shards concreted atop the wall as they tried to get over. He'd seen them actual dying out there from being crushed, and that well before his own offside boot had travelled the lethal half inch from the position where it was held at this present moment. Which was right close to the master trap bolt.

All this while, as he'd been ruminating on the big days of the past, he had kept half an eye cocked on the big bay window which jutted from the second storey of the courthouse. There was an indistinct figure stood behind the glass there which seemed to fill even that large space. For Judge Parker was in all ways a big man.

No one who was near to the federal executioner in those tense moments of crowd hush was able to observe the little fellow's thin and bewhiskered face. The three McCrackens were certainly in no state to observe it, blindered as they were and with their evil minds in any case presumably set on other concerns. And as for Colonel Hall, the U.S. marshal who had previously read out their warrants, he was now stood with the back of his trim Chesterfield held toward Maledon, facing the crowd with his fedora in his hand and his well groomed head lowered. The other McCrackens who'd been allowed to climb up and take the relatives' bench at the back were also not watching him, them being all female and snivelling fit to take in nothing but their own grief. So apart from the more distant eyes of the crowd the court hangman had no others upon him just then.

If anyone had been studying him close up they would have seen a strange contradiction in his expression. On the one hand, he obviously shared the common and basically humane impatience of the majority in the square that the delay should be over and done with. But side by side with that normalcy there coexisted a look that was nothing short of slavish adoration in his deepset and slightly pouched eyes, as they were now concentrated absolutely on the occupant of the bay window.

Up there, at the highest position of all, Isaac Parker had once again taken his familiar stance beside a tall oaken lectern. A Bible lay open on the lectern, and one of the judge's large hands was set lightly upon it.

Behind him was the principal room of his private chambers above the courtroom, the walls lined with law books but with only a modest-looking desk across one corner. On the floor was a single rather threadbare rug. A portrait of Mary Parker, his wife, and their two boys Charles and James, was prominent on the desk. The bay window itself had been specially reglazed at the judge's own instruction. The original glass in it when he had first come to the town back in 1875 had permitted too much distracting (and sometimes upsetting) sound to enter his room. Now it was replaced with thick greenhouse glass.

Looking down through that now at the great twelve man hanging machine, he was able to feel detached in a physical sense from what his eyes were steadfastly regarding. For Parker was no simple sadist. He watched all such executions because he saw himself as the earthly representative of the Almighty, whose will had been violated by those merciless sub-creatures down there on the gibbet. In that solemn capacity he had to watch. But naturally he had no base wish to hear their dying screams. And neither did he wish to hear the unpleasantly savage sounds that the crowds often made on those grave occasions; sounds that might have indicated even to his resolute mind that the didactic message of the executions was sometimes ineffective.

He had never needed to tell George

Maledon that he should watch for his ultimate signal. It was just something that had grown to be understood between them during their fifteen years of joint devotion to the cause of justice.

Sometimes, despite the partial insulation from events which the window afforded him, he did become aware of the impatience of those below. But he steadfastly refused to share it. Instead he tried to give over his mind to a stern reappraisal of the degree of guilt incurred by those wretches presently below him, who were about to meet their Maker. It did not seem unreasonable to him that those who had committed particularly vile crimes should be required to wait proportionately longer than those who had not.

The McCracken brothers stood about midway on the judge's scale as to their degree of vileness. So it was not much longer now before he dipped his grey-white head almost imperceptibly and

George Maledon kicked the trapbolt.

Once the act of atonement was performed, Parker slid to his knees and began praying; deeply felt prayer that was offered up not for the souls of the departed, for he regarded them as now passed beyond the jurisdiction of himself and his court. But always and solely on behalf of their victims.

* * *

That evening, resting after his supper in the easy chair in his living room, George Maledon was smoking his clay pipe and reading a copy of the *Elevator*. Nearby in the kitchen he could hear his wife and daughter doing the dishes and swapping woman talk.

Neither Eunice nor Annie had said as much as a word to him during the recent family repast. They never did on his work days. For Eunice Maledon held an independent viewpoint on capital punishment that diverged very considerably from her husband's. It

7

was said that she ruled the hangman's household with a rod of iron, and never let him speak about his job when within his own four walls. And neither would she speak to him for the rest of whichever day it might be when he had once again taken life.

He had gotten used to that attitude over the years, though it still gravelled him that his own little angel Annie had picked it up from her ma as she got her growth. It seemed hard to him that a man's trade should be held against him by his own kin. Though he was fair-minded enough to allow that things were never easy for a hangman's family. Some of the books he owned on the fine old art made it plain he wasn't the first neck stretcher to have family troubles. Folks tended to shun the operator and his whole tribe in case they were somehow tainted with evil; when of course the truth was he did it solely for Isaac Parker and the Good Lord both.

But it was no use reasoning with

your average hog ignorant public folks. He'd found that out long ago. The job was just a cross that the whole Maledon family had to tote between them on their way to Calvary. And for his part he shouldered that burden willingly enough. Like he reminded the other two pretty often, it put steady bread in their bellies.

After all, he reflected now, as he tasted stale tobacco and leaned down to tip dottle on to the nearby hearthstone, *I am the goddam Prince of my kind*. Even those lousy eastern newspapermen who were forever trying to pull the judge down had been forced to own that he was hanging's top hand. Though it was a Saint Lou paper that had first given him the Prince tag. *PRINCE OF HANGMEN* was the header that paper had carried on the big day when he'd opened it out and felt an odd quiver inside, as he used his finger to read down the several columns that were all about him.

Of course that newspaper story

hadn't been all pure admiration. In fact, there were bits of it that were total unfounded. But at least they'd given him that right smart name and now he was known by it nationwide. And then the rope dealership had come his way once he had the name, and the slogan those fellows up to Chicago had paid him to use: *If it's strong enough for Maledon it's strong enough for you.* Which had seen to it that a bit more bread went in the family's bellies.

But the trouble with that publicity was it had set off a string of copiers. Fellows who made out they had the same gift for it. Fellows like that Zeb Allen over in Philly, who set theirselves up with half a dozen sticks banged together and figured that put them there overnight with the Prince of them all.

A hard grin touched his beard-fringed lips as he began repacking the pipe bowl. He was recollecting what had happened to Zeb that time when he himself fell ill and the fool government hired that jackleg to come down and try his hand on the twelve-man-er. Goddam gut-puking disaster all round, that's what had happened . . .

Having now mused himself back into a fair humor again after the way those two had given him the silent treatment at supper, he sucked heartily through the pipe at a sulphur match and then settled down to catch up with the latest town doings in the *Elevator*.

Usually there was nothing that ruffled him in that paper's columns. The editor was both a staunch friend of Judge Parker and an equally staunch pro-hanger. In fact his publication was required reading for all of the Parker faction in the city, and Maledon allowed no other to cross his threshold. (For he wouldn't let the women boss him over a thing like that.)

There were as many as four Fort Smith newspapers in print by that date. Two were nominally free of interest, the *Elevator* supported Parker, and the *Independent* was the distinctly muffled mouthpiece for those few hardy souls in western Arkansas who believed in Change. But in fact the papers stood three to one in favor of the judge.

So the handling of such local and national affairs that he now perused did nothing at first to dispel his improved mood. But he was about to turn a page to the baseball scores when, to his amazement, a certain name leapt at him from the bold print; a name that had chanced to be on his mind just a few minutes before. The header in question read:

ZEBEDIAH ALLEN INHERITS HANG-LAND'S DUKEDOM!

And underneath that his bugging eyes encountered:

It is reliably reported from the East that Philadelphia's well known exponent of the ancient art has recently 'pulled off' no mean achievement. Operating with a specially constructed gallows made to his own design, Allen on June 4th this year despatched a convicted rapist in ten seconds precisely, timed from when the fleet-footed executioner was standing on Mother Earth at the base of his contraption until the condemned hit the noose.

This feat, if accurate, surely poses a threat to the vaunted supremacy of our well known local citizen George Maledon. In fact, without seeking to incur opprobrium for facetiousness while dilating upon such a 'grave subject' this correspondent cannot forbear to pose the question: must our neighborhood Prince now give precedence to this new Hanging Duke? — which title, we understand, has now been bestowed upon him by our sister Press along the Atlantic seaboard.

There was some more of it too, and done in the same smart ass style. God dammit he just couldn't *believe* this shit was carried in the *Elevator*! He wondered what the Old Man would have to say about it to his dining pal Teddy Falkirk when he got to read it his own self! There was one editor who'd find himself run out of Arkansas on a postoak unless he missed his guess! It was *downright total outrage* for shit like this to be carried in a paper calling itself strong for true justice! Why, he'd go round himself first thing in the morning to their office on Third and give them his own piece of mind for a start! *And* he'd make damn sure they read this where it counted in the courthouse! *And* he'd see about suing them for blaspheming his own name!

Gradually he cooled down. Although it would be more accurate to say that he cooled down in so far as the article had affected his general sense of propriety. Where it had affected his professional standing, though, his anger was now on the increase.

That damn upstart Zeb setting himself above him again! Treating

*a serious matter like a hanging as
though he was some crooked eastern
jockey in a starting gate*

And anyhow, that story was sure
as hell all newspaper bull juice. He
knew better than anyone else it just
wasn't possible to shin up nine steps
and see to a subject so as he would
hit the noose in only ten flat. It just
couldn't be done, even if you were the
world's best hangman and the world's
best trackstar both.

. . . Unless, of course, that Zeb had
gone and knocked himself up an illegal
lynching box with only four steps up or
something like . . . Yep, he wouldn't
put that past him. Zeb wouldn't care
worth a durn if he had to put a bullet
in the subject after or pull on his legs
or whatever — just as long as he could
claim this speed record and that plumb
ridiculous title with it! The Hanging
Duke for Christ's sake . . . it even
sounded jackleg in itself. It just had no
natural dignity to it whatever as a title.
Why, there wasn't nobody in the whole

wide continent as wouldn't know the jigger who'd claim a cheapskate title like that must be the lousiest, rottenest shyster that ever . . .

But slowly it was borne in on him, even at the molten height of his fury, that Zeb's gibbet must have worked a bit better than he'd given credit for. Even the eastern Press wouldn't have failed to mention it if that speed-hanging had ended in the nightmare that haunted all executioners everywhere: the nightmare of a Second Try.

So somehow or other then Zeb had managed it straight . . .

That farther thought was more than maddening — it was deeply worrysome.

And it was all *Isaac's* goddam fault when you came down to it. Forever stringing things out from his window to punish the subjects, so there was never any call for speedwork. Elsewise there would never have been any question that he could outclass one like Allen in that department, as well as in all the others . . .

He gradually became aware that Eunice had come through with a stack of cleaned plates and had set them down on the kitchen table beside him. And she was no longer acting tight lipped toward him either. Her round face above the plump body was full of concern and she was saying:

" . . . something the matter with you tonight? You look a bit funny George."

He glowered up at her half-seeingly. "Funny enough to make you find your tongue woman, uh?" he grunted thickly. Then he added more to himself:

"Oh yes somethin' is the matter all right. And I ain't about to let it lay, oh no." He lurched up from the easy chair and headed for the door.

"Where are you off to now?" she called after him.

"My workshop," he replied dourly.

2

OVER the years, George Maledon's old stable building had become one of the famous sights of the town; though few had actually seen it. But those who had been allowed inside there had spread the word; and had sometimes garbled the word somewhat fantastically in the process. Not that there was any need for exaggeration, for the reality was not short on dramatic impact.

Certainly none of the hordes of tourists who were drawn into town at peak times via the riverboats or the railroad station had been let in there, though several had tried to bribe their way in. For Maledon was only bribable on a superficial level where his life's work was concerned. He had no objection to letting those yokels who'd come in for the executions keep his beer stein filled up in Fort Smith's many bars and taverns, and in return he would dish out a few well-worn accounts of hangings past. But as for their present trips, he made it bluntly clear that it was only the action itself in the square they would get to see, and none of the patient professional skill that lay behind it.

The converted stable lay a few feet across the dooryard from his house on North Thirteenth Street. He had replaced the two big carriage doors midway of one of the long walls with a line of centre windows, but kept the half doors on an end wall as the workshop's entrance. And he had left a part of the upper tallet floor still in place in order to store his supplies of fresh untreated rope and, latterly, the overflow of the Collection. Otherwise the single large room was open to the rafters.

From some of those rafters he had rigged a pulley system, on which stretch out his ready prepared and custom made ropes on sandbags. An adjustable centre lamp was also suspended, casting a large pool of light down upon his workbench. Near the bench were a couple of slap up bookshelves on one of the few bare areas of calcimined inner wall; for Maledon was surprisingly unhandy as a domestic carpenter. The shelves supported his specialist library consisting of about a dozen volumes. Some were old and foreign and rare, and to get them he had spent more than he could afford to an eastern mailbook company.

But of course it wasn't those humdrum details which had made the stable talked about. It was the Collection that folks wanted to gape at and shudder over.

The Collection was indeed somewhat uncommon. It consisted of line upon line of cockling daguerreotype squares, each one proudly recording a subject's one and only appearance on the nightmarish Fort Smith hanging machine. By

20

now they almost covered the whole of the available space from floor to ceiling, and the machine's operative had regretfully begun to store portraits of the more routine badmen who came his way upstairs on the hay floor, undisplayed.

But all the big names he'd handled were prominently on view, together with the neatly coiled nooses pegged underneath which related to each one. For Maledon had a superstition about not using the same rope twice. Many of the daguerreotypes bore pencilled additions of abstruse technical comment, albeit often expressed in homespun terms.

He was usually most meticulous about keeping the Collection right up to date, and but for the great shock he had just sustained from the *Elevator* by now he would probably be busying himself with pasting up the three McCrackens to join the rest. But in this present emergency he abandoned all thoughts of routine.

He reached for his lamp and pulled it down and fired it up; then slumped dispiritedly below it in his battered old cane chair behind the workbench.

The lamp began to hiss companionably in the workshop's secluded silence. Now and then a carriage would grind by on North Thirteenth, and a bulleting wind between the house and the stable occasionally rattled the half doors. But otherwise he was sealed off inside with his boding night thoughts.

"No I just can't feature how," he mumbled aloud at the facing wall of dimly glistening likenesses, in the self-communing manner of one who was often by himself. "Iffen that cheap trickster's really done it like the paper said, then I've got to own I'm licked off the board. Damn it all, I've nothin' to go on. T'ain't as if I'd got a diagram of his lynchin' box as I could break down and study on. I know one thing though — I ain't about to crawl to the so-called Hanging Duke asking him to send a diagram of whatever it is he slung up to do it on."

He lapsed then for some moments into a dejected silence. But his words had set off a thought-track in his brain which presently brightened him up some. He reached to pull out a drawer from the workbench, resuming his droning commentary as he did so.

"But what I *have* still got somewheres is the blueprint for the old twelve-man-er hisself. That paper I drawed up back in 'Seventy-five after Isaac first got the notion of buildin' a big gibbet for example hangin's. Goddam thing must still be in here somewheres . . . Ah! Here he is . . . "

He unfolded the original plan for the hanging machine; doing so with a certain priestly reverence despite the wholly practical turn of his present thoughts.

Yes. It was all here done out in sections as he now remembered doing it. He remembered that he'd tried to make it as much like a regular arkipet style blueprint as he could.

The four tree sized corner baulks (which had proved damned hard to find too. They'd had to send out of state for those big boles). The right ambitious twenty foot platform. The nineteen and a half feet of trap (which had binded in spite of all the grease in Arkansas, and there'd been all those foulups on the early trials until he'd seen it had to split into three separate traps). That was the kind of difficulty which didn't show up on a slick diagram — but sure as hell did show up when you worked a gibbet live.

Now his eye fell affectionately on the in-scale giant crossbeam, which made even those fat corners look like matchsticks. Featuring its dozen rope slots — unlike in any other gallows he'd ever seen, in or out of a book. That scheme had just come to him in the drawing, in a sort of pure flash of invention. And although them slots had been thought up in theory in the first place, they had always worked just fine for him in practise too. No problems with windage and no problems with body sway. As long as you bethought to keep your grease tin topped up they were a subject's best friend, them slots were . . . "

Then there was the standard nine-stepper up to it all. Again in solid wood on the plan, and angled steepish to make sure it crossed the height up to the platform. No chance for any fancy piece of inventioning there, of course. The law laid it down to be nine steps minimum — and it surely wasn't an ass to either. For like he'd figured straight off when reading that shit about Allen just now, you couldn't legally aim to bring the time down by having a low platform and a short ladder.

He wondered suddenly if that was how Zeb had finagled it — through knocking up a special four-stepper, or somesuch illegal height, and then gone hunting for some elephant-sized subject whose column would break in just a few feet of drop. Yep, he wouldn't mind betting that was the cheap and cheating way it had been done. That way Zeb could have aimed to short the time on getting hisself up there, and also short the time it took the subject to get down. Ten secs became near about possible done that away, if they were leg-strapped first . . .

"But you're a different article from that altogether, ain't you old son," he now addressed the paper in his hands. "Wasn't no question of speed coming into it when I fashioned you in my mind. Was plenty difficult enough to make you reliable to handle your capacity shipment, without no speed stunts in the bargain."

He took his pipe from his mouth and hawked expressively on the stable's cobbles; then sat there a while longer deep in thought, trying to figure a way how the damned thing might be quickened. For iffen it *could* somehow be quickened, just temporary, then God damn it he could maybe best Zeb Allen a dozen times over and with no cheap tricks involved neither . . .

But no. It was sheerly impossible to hang any man in ten seconds on a proper legal gibbet, like he'd known it was in the first place. He put the old blueprint back in the drawer and raised one of his thick-skinned hands to cap the hot lamp chimney before craning his neck to blow out the flame.

Totally defeated, and more depressed than ever, he re-crossed the yard and went to bed.

★ ★ ★

But things seemed a whole lot better by morning.

One improvement was the fact that Eunice and Annie were talking to him again at breakfast. And as there were no engagements for today in his hanging book, it seemed he could look forward to having a normal sociable evening too when he got home from the jail after spelling the Death Row turnkeys; which was still expected of him on his free-of-subjects days, even though he had gotten famous now. The way the bigwigs in Washington saw it he was still just a common deputy U.S. marshal assigned to the jail, like he'd been before the judge raised him up from that low station to become the Prince of Hangmen.

That title seemed much more secure to him this morning than it had seemed last night. He'd scanned that piece in the *Elevator* again over his bacon, and in the light of day it was plumb obvious no one would take a stupid caper like that seriously. The whole antic had just been bragged up by Zeb and a few hack newspapermen. He'd been dumb to pay it any mind whatever, and from here on he surely wouldn't.

However, that firm resolve was not destined to last long. On his usual half-hour walk to court that morning, a young lad on roller skates passed him on the hill down Garrison Avenue, yelling: "How about the duke then, Maledon?" as he flashed past.

Well naturally he didn't get in a stew again over a little happening like that. In a way, it sort of confirmed his new sensible viewpoint that the notion of a speed hanging was too stupid to interest an adult type mind. If some of the local kids planned to ride him over it, well, they rode him plenty over his line of work anyway so he was used to that by now. There was hardly a day in his life went by when some kid wouldn't shout out at him smart ass stuff like:

'Hangerman, hangerman, don't you hang me, 'cause I don't aim to wear these boots for all Eternity'

No he wouldn't let those fool kids get to him over it.

But that new calm viewpoint took a more marked sag when he branched off from Garrison on to Sixth Street, before heading for the court buildings as usual on Third.

He was making the detour because he hadn't got round yet this month to signing his picturemaker's chit before it went for payment to the court clerk. Hal Rathbone did him a fairly good job for the stingy federal rate he was paid, and he knew it could be poor business to make him wait for it in the bargain.

He turned off the street by Rathbone's shingle design of a camera with a big concertina lens, and went inside. The narrow lobby was empty, so he rang the handbell on the counter and then studied the unromantic features of Grover Cleveland, which were displayed on one wall surrounded by Hal's trade shots of blooming new-wedded local couples. Then the picturemaker twitched aside his darkroom flap and came through to him.

"Oh it's you George," he said without any great enthusiasm. Although he needed his government checks, Maledon was aware that taking the official likenesses of condemned rapists and killers was not his chosen work. None of the town's photographers were keen on it.

"Look, I'm sorry I never got to the jail yesterday to take that Choctaw you mentioned," Rathbone went on apologetically. "I did mean to but — "

"Don't fret, that one'll keep a bit," Maledon told him with a laconic arm wave. "He ain't scheduled to go till we can make up more of a team again. The judge allus likes 'em to go on a team drop without they're some account by theirselves. Elsewise he reckons they don't make a big enough example. Like no one had heard anythin' of that Choctaw before he upped and knifed his mother. Did that one go off by hisself he'd never pull in more than say twenty yokels for it. And that would be no use at all far as the judge is concerned."

Hal Rathbone swallowed and nodded. He was tall and thin and balding, though still young. When he swallowed, his Adam's apple rose prominently above his celluloid collar and made him look very nervous. Which he often was when around George Maledon and his violent subjects. He was now reminded of a particular cause of that nervousness.

"Look George, I've been meaning to say for some time I'd prefer it if we went back to me taking them one by one in their cells again. I just can't feel easy when I have to take them when they're in that exercise pen. I know they're often chained, and the jailers are always armed, but I still don't admire taking them if they ain't penned apart. And Joanne feels the same way about it," he finished firmly.

"Women do get fractious and peculiar if a man has aught to do with killers and such," Maledon replied with a certain ruefulness in his tone. He eyed the picturemaker shrewdly over his jutting pipe. "Pity about them McCracken shots," he murmured, apparently veering off the point.

"What was wrong with them?" Rathbone demanded with another nervous throat jump. "I thought they came out well enough or I wouldn't have sent them round to you."

"Like I've told you before you don't include enough neck on them," the executioner grumbled. "I had just the same trouble when I used Sy Needham before you. What you'd ought to remember is I don't want them as standard pictures. I want them to study on before I go to work, and also as a permanent record after. That means you can miss out all you want above their ears, for what I care. But I need to have their goddam necks included way down past collar-line. And you see the buggers loose their collars too."

He paused, and puffed smoke reflectively over the photographer's counter. "I dunno, Hal, I'm sure I don't know," he resumed sadly. "If the likenesses don't come out just right, and now you're settin' conditions about how you'll take 'em in the first place — well, I'm scared I'll just have to use Needham again for it, even though he wasn't none too satisfactory either."

"All right all right, I'll take them how you want," Rathbone said hastily. "And where you want, if it's that damn important."

"Well that's what I call co-operative Hal," Maledon told him warmly. "Right co-operative. Saves me from a sight of unlockin' if you shoot 'em in the bullpen. Now what I've come round for is I ain't signed your chitty yet for last month. I'll do it now if it's ready."

When the photographer came back with the account slip his resentment had had time to resurface. He said balefully: "I saw the piece in the *Elevator* last night, George. Seems this fellow Allen is in a way of being a pretty hot rival of yours. Did you see it?"

The hangman's brown teeth had clamped tightly around his pipe stem. But he made a big try at giving a light answer.

"I might have just glanced at it on my way to the scores. Yes, now you mention it I recall I did just happen to glance at it." He forced a croaking laugh. "Believe me, Hal, the so-called hangman in question ain't much."

Hal Rathbone wasn't fooled. His face showed that in every smirkish line.

"Is that a fact? The way the paper told it he's a big number back East," he said unpleasantly. "Where it counts, I guess."

George Maledon ground at his clay pipe until he was in danger of chewing it through. He cast around in his raging mind for something effective to come back at the photographer with.

"This here chit of yours," he spat out finally. "I hope you ain't tryin' to slide too much past the new court clerk we've got since Adams was retired off the job. This Crawford Higgs bucko has been questioning the extra expenses all over. Just thought I'd warn you in friendly fashion, Hal," he told him with a matching baleful grin.

"I'm not sliding anything past him," the young picturemaker protested hotly. "Every last shot I've sent round to your creepy shed can be tallied up if that's needful — and I don't appreciate you suggesting it can't!"

"Slack off, son," he grunted, while signing his name to the slip with a suitable flourish. "Never suggested no such thing. I'll have some more for you to do on Murder Row sometime tomorrow forenoon — iffen that's convenient a course," he finished up with a final barbed grin.

★ ★ ★

He hadn't been entirely bull-shitting the boy about Isaac's awkward new clerk of court. Of late, he himself had sorely missed the more easy-going attitude to incidental expenses shown by Charlie Adams, the former clerk. There were certain costs which he and the court undertaker were in the habit of arriving at between them, during joint discussion, before presenting them for payment at the courthouse. Both he and the undertaker had been somewhat taken aback by the new clerk's clear lack of trust in such figuring.

And what made that specially provoking was the way word had already gone around the town that Crawford Higgs would spend out on himself like a blamed emperor when he went on The Row, which he often did. It seemed to be only his fellow officers of the court that he liked to keep away from temptation.

The executioner's gloom had now returned to him in full measure after the way that kid on the street, and now the picturemaker, had both known all about that shitty story in the *Elevator*. He was sure now that he would soon find all the turnkeys in the jail would make a point of telling him about it too. Not to mention what the no-account ordinary prisoners would cat-call at him, when he passed their cages as usual on his way up to Murder Row.

Both those fears proved entirely justified.

3

JUDGE PARKER reached for his gavel at around six o'clock that evening.

That was a remarkably early hour for him to recess a second session. The United States District Court of and for the Western District of Arkansas and the Indian Territories was always convened sharp on eight-thirty in the morning, and it often sat until far into the night. Only Christmas Day and the Sabbath were exempted from the jurist's religious fervor for dispensing justice; which had, if anything, increased with the passage of his fifteen years on the federal bench.

Some of the people in his courtroom looked puzzled over the early recess; more particularly those who occupied the public area, and their more colorful additions on the recently installed long seat at the back, which had been dubbed 'Beauty's Row' by the less sober elements of the local Press. But J. Warren Reed, the experienced counselor who was acting for the defense in this present murder trial, understood the reason for it perfectly.

Reed had just been getting to the nub of his main address to the court. In its earlier stages he had savagely demolished much of the evidence against his client, a sullen young full-blood Cherokee named Calvin Rainbird. Judge Parker had intervened on at least six occasions while Reed had striven to do that, but despite His Honor's best and sternest efforts it was becoming plain that the men in the jury box were being swayed by the lawyer's eloquence.

Hence this early adjournment, Reed reflected sourly, as he gathered up his papers and donned his clawhammer frock coat and fashionably shortened silk hat, in readiness to return to his office.

He was well aware that by tomorrow the adroit old sinshouter in the high chair would have thought up some fresh ploy to obtain a conviction — and, of course, more bait for the great hanging machine outside. And the smug face of the chief government prosecutor, William H. Clayton, who stood beside the other table across the aisle from Reed, reflected that anticipation of events.

But in fact Reed's departure was delayed a few moments longer. Isaac Parker was in fact extremely vexed to have been forced to lose several hours of good court time due to the jurymen's stupid rejection of his guidance. So, as soon as the gavel had struck the cherrywood in front of him, he proceeded to admonish both them and Lawyer Reed in no uncertain terms before he let them leave.

"Rarely in my three lustrums of service upon this bench," he led off in the familiar booming tones, "have I been forced to listen to such a farrago of half-truth and distortion as that volunteered by the learned counselor who has just spoken." And here he paused to shoot a withering blue firebolt of contempt at Warren Reed.

"I will deal with those several errors of fact and interpretation tomorrow, before we proceed any farther with this trial. And meanwhile (here the blue firebolt was switched more generally at the jury box) I would commend those who are here to deliver their verdict before the Almighty and this court, that they should seek to distinguish between pettifogging trickery, the pursuance of truth and justice, and the proper performance of their duty! And I would commend them also to study the countenance of the prisoner in the dock — as I have done at length — and take note of the open villainy that is writ large upon it! I would urge them to recall the words of the witness who knew this craven beast from his earliest youth — and who may be

41

supposed to have a somewhat more profound knowledge of him than has his indulgent representative! — those damning words which I noted down and now repeat to you gentlemen, for your overnight consideration.

"I quote: *He always was a quick tempered son of . . .* ahem. That sense is clear enough. *And I would not trust him nohow when he was sniffing around my wife or my baby sister even.*

"There speaks the voice of one who knows him well, and who did not seek to denigrate the companion of his youth any more unduly or severely than the ghastly deed of this case warranted — nay, demanded before God! And I finally commend you to consider the prisoner's own afflicted spouse, who appeared so poignantly before you, and her total and admirable frankness regarding his former procession of savage infidelities which were paraded before her own virtue, and which culminated in this act of sheer depravity which brings him to this place of atonement now.

"Gentlemen, you will give your most serious and sober attention to these matters — perhaps more than previously — before we reconvene at eight-thirty tomorrow morning."

★ ★ ★

After climbing the stairs to his chambers, Parker irritably cast off his robe as he entered the outer office there, draping it carelessly over a chair back.

"Ah, Higgs," he said then, beckoning. "Would you come through please for a moment?"

The suit which the court robe had revealed had been made by a Washington tailor, and once it had cost the then young Congressman rather more than he could afford. But that time was now far distant, and the suit had become worn and shiny. Similarly, the leather of his shoes were cracked above and much mended below. But he was still a most impressive and daunting figure, weighing not much under three hundred pounds and standing a ramrod-straight six feet. His skin was still pink and his hair still thick, and still combed indifferently to the side away from the right hand parting; but now, along with his chin beard, it had gone as white as wool from the stress of his years of running the toughest court on the frontier; which he firmly believed it still was.

Once, as a brilliant younger lawyer in the Capital, he had earned large sums of money. But not since coming to Arkansas. For it was a strange anomaly of the economics of the federal court that its presiding judge was paid less than the person who had just followed him into his room.

Crawford Higgs was a thickset youngish man with an always pale and damp and glistening face. He wore nose glasses, and expensive broadcloth of a cut which made the judge's suiting look still more threadbare and old-fashioned than it was. He had a set of dark brown eyes that were uncomfortably steady in their focusing, and slightly magnified by the skimpy gold-rimmed lenses.

The court clerk had been transferred to Fort Smith from the government penitentiary in Ohio, along with a solid reputation for cost cutting and general efficiency. Before departing from there he had been told privately and bluntly to get some sense into the Fort Smith funding; though he did not regard his new post as anything more than 'a jerkwater stop-off' on the smooth and fast journey of his career in government service, and had been heard to say as much when relaxing in the town.

But Judge Parker knew nothing of any of that. He was far too unworldly to feel jealousy or any other kind of emotion — or even interest — toward his replacement clerk of court. Now seating himself at his simple plain-cut desk, he was still entirely taken up with the unsatisfactory proceedings he had just adjourned.

"Higgs, it is not going as it should downstairs," he began, with his scorching blue gaze now turned inward rather than at the standing clerk. He tented his large fingers on the desk's leather inset panel, pressing them together with some force. "I have done what I can to delay, but that confounded fellow Reed will win it unless the evidence can be, ahem, greatly strengthened. I think we had better get that missionary fellow back from Tahlequah in a hurry. The one who first found the corpses in that condition. I think perhaps he can be induced to — "

But then, to his astonishment, the new clerk cut firmly across his instruction.

"Well, I don't know, Judge," he said oddly, rubbing at the sweat along his lank flaxen hairline. "A rail voucher to Tahlequah — a *second* voucher back and forth to Tahlequah — can it really be justified in fiscal terms?"

Isaac Parker looked at him directly, in extreme surprise. It was the first time since his arrival that he had taken the time or trouble to do that. Once over his surprise, he said coldly:

"You can leave me to decide that I think. Send the voucher off to him by the next train, and also send the fellow a wire that I shall require him to be in the city by two p.m. at the latest. Oh, and when he arrives, have a bailiff meet him at the depot to escort him straight to my room here. That account of his must be put to the jury in, ah, rather more lurid and persuasive terms, as I must explain to him beforehand."

Crawford Higgs regarded his new chief thoughtfully with his impenetrable brown gaze. Before quitting Ohio, he had heard all manner of tales about this leftover Hanging Judge they still had down in Arkansas, who was so hot for convictions that he would do most anything to get them.

The talk he'd just had with him seemed to confirm the truth of that. And plainly the judge himself was not going to accept the slightest financial restrictions on his freedom of movement.

But then it didn't really matter what his personal reaction was to such restrictions. It was their effect on lesser mortals that concerned Ohio and Washington, as Crawford Higgs could now understand more completely.

His small thin mouth assumed a compliant smile. "Just as you say, Judge. Will that be all now?"

★ ★ ★

Later, at home in the town cottage he had taken, the new court clerk had his feet up in the livingroom. He was reading a new tome he'd brought south with him, entitled *Business and the Legislative*, while occasionally swapping a remark with his wife.

"I don't think it will take long to get this over and done with," he told her now. "Just as well, too. I'd go crazy if I had to kick my heels in this burg for much longer."

Lurleen Higgs looked up from her dime romance with an expression on her face that was slightly cynical. "I gathered from the woman over the fence that you've discovered how to make your spare time here not entirely boring, dear," she said with a touch of acid.

The clerk's confident expression took a slight sag. He forced a laugh. "Oh," he said then. "That sparked off some gossip, did it, my little errand to the tenderloin district? You should know by now that there are certain offices connected with the job that I can't delegate — especially to the bunch of prairie clowns in Parker's court. There's some matters I have to attend to myself in all conscience."

The face of the youngish southern widow whom Crawford Higgs had married did not show a vastly greater degree of trust while she considered that answer. And her tone hadn't altered much either when she said:

"I know that, dear. I know that

well enough. Just mind you don't feel conscientious too often."

★ ★ ★

It was funny the way the answer came to him. About an hour after he thought he'd given up on it final. After he'd tried this that and the other and all useless the same, and he'd said to the blamed machine out loud:

"All right, you bastard, you won't never do it fast for me will you? There's just no making you work any different from how I made you work in the first place. You've got me flat beat and you know it don't you?"

And then he had angrily turned his back on the gibbet, and gone stomping across the square to the jail to pick a work detail to freshen up the machine for its next custom presently. And damned if it wasn't them no-account penny ante criminals theirselves who led him to find the answer!

It came about when he was chousing

the end of the work gang up the ladder of the machine, digging at his yellow-shirted back to encourage him with one of his double pistols. That convict was bigger than most, and lazier too, and he was slow and awkward with the weight of a large and full pail of lye soap in one of his black hands, and a couple of flailing brooms in the other.

"Quit foolin' and git on up!" the executioner advised him, with another corrective pistol jab at his spine. "Like I allus say, you damn nigger-Creeks are the worst workers on God's earth. Why I went and chosed you for it, Mr Rufus Davis sir, I'm blamed if I know. *I said git on up, you varmint!*"

"Look, I'm tryin' to, Maledon," the breed protested. "Have you ever tried totin' anything but your death-dealin' self up these steps? An amateur made pitch of steps like this to go up means it's got to be taken slow, without you aim to see this pailful all slopped down 'em and gone nowhere near where the piss and puke's at."

"*You hobble your lip!*" he croaked at the convict on a furious high pitch, raising his pistol now to crack him with it on his crinkly-covered skull. "Who in Tophet d'you think you're talkin' to, you common crim'nal? Do you want me fix it so's you get another year stuck on your pull? You git up above with the rest in double quick time or — "

But then he cut off his reedy croaking and lowered the handgun uncertainly, and stared at the impassive misbegot offender with the pail.

"What's this shit about my ladder?" he said in a slightly altered tone. "What do you know callin' it amacher? Was you some kind of rawhide carpenter before you went bad, Davis?"

"Sure I was, and not rawhide neither," the big breed rumbled. "Had my own business with my brother up at Tulsy. But then I had this trouble with a loan and —

"I'm not interested in hearing your court pitch, you dumb idiot! I am mebbe just the slightest bit possibly interested, though, in how you *think* you'd improve these steps of mine."

He colored beneath his bush of beard as he made that unfitting admission, and the words came out of him like pulled teeth. "*Well? How?*" he demanded, back to full croak again.

Davis scratched thoughtfully at one of his large denim-clad haunches. He propped the soap pail on a step, in a leisurely style that would have drawn a torrent of further abuse from the hangman under normal circumstances. Now, however, apart from a choked-off turkey gobble, he showed for him amazing restraint when dealing with an insolent non-capital prisoner.

"The first thing I'd do is box in these gaps like regular stairs," Davis said, motioning at the space beneath the rung where the pail was tilted. "Taken together with the silly pitch of it, anyone who goes up in a hurry is apt to break a leg through one of those gaps. It's odd you ain't done that yourself, you being the only one

53

in the steady habit of goin' up," he added dryly.

"Then I guess what I'd do is pull out this clumsy banged-on frame, which would be easy enough since it ain't 'tailed on. Then I'd splice more length on the bottom. Then you could haze us fellows up and down as fast as you liked, and it would be safe to."

"Would it now," George Maledon sneered. "And so doin' you'd go above nine steps. I guess a lunkhead saw jockey like you wouldn't know, but in my perfession the law holds out for nine steps minimum."

Davis shrugged. "Does it hold out for nine steps maximum is more the point, I'd say."

The executioner stared at him for a long moment without voicing another word. Then he murmured: "Look Davis — you don't admire cleanin' up the gibbet, right?"

The halfbreed shrugged again. "Who does? You gettin' concerned about my wishes, hangerman? Well now, ain't that wonderful."

George Maledon let that unrespectful comment go by him as well. He turned away and hollered to those above them, who were now sluicing and brushing water across the platform:

"Hey you, McLish — jump down and take up his bucket. I'm holding you responsible for seein' the others do a good job this time — specially on that stain by stall five what you last lot of buggers never got out. And don't go thinkin' I won't still have my eye on you, since I'm only goin' round the corner a minute to the woodshed."

He had led Davis to the shed in question, where various rough-cut timber was stacked against two of the walls. "Can you see anything here, you could use to splice on some extra like you said?

The burly breed began to squeeze himself through the tangles of wood. Although his blunt face was still held in rigid lines of boredom and resignation, Maledon sensed the dulled pleasure it gave him to be with timber again. "Well?" he said impatiently.

"There a couple lengths here would match the ladder frame close enough," Davis said a moment later. "And I could break up that milk box and use the clad for stopping those gaps — and maybe this here for the treads . . . "

He peered through the dust he'd raised at the hangman by the shed door, with a definite spark of life now discernible in his black-twice-over eyes. "You got tools for it somewheres, Maledon?"

"I've got tools," he answered with a sudden rush of hope.

4

OF course he'd known that wasn't all there was to it by a considerable piece. For one thing, he was no champion pacer and never had been. He knew he'd have to work out pretty hard with a skip-rope to get his feet quickened enough to dash up the longer ladder the way he'd need to to break the record.

And even if he managed to get that quick, there was still the difficulty of the master bolt being placed midway of the platform. That was worth four damned seconds in itself, just to get from the side of the platform to the master bolt.

And of course he couldn't use deputies to ready the subjects for him either. Did he do that, Zeb Allen would be able to claim a foul. He had a nightmare vision of himself fixing their blinders on at truly blinding speed . . . The feeling of hope in him began to wither some.

It did not take the ex-carpenter long to alter the steps as he had suggested. And a coat of pitch over the whole flight made the added two treads blend in unnoticeably. But that extra length, plus the safer feel of the infills all the way up, made a sight of difference to how you could climb them. Hope began to well back again a bit.

After he had taken the detail back to the jail he returned alone to the gibbet, and gave the re-made steps a first trial. Even without hurrying any more than usual, he reckoned he'd clipped off about two seconds just from the new ease of slope.

Then he had to postpone all further speed experiments, for a single subject was due to go at three, and he had to break off and do all the standard preparation for that.

Like most of the single drops he handled these days, this one had a Name. Luckey July was what the discriminating Prince of Hangmen thought of as a fairly big number; and, in fact, July pulled in a respectable total of two and a half thousand spectators before the crowd started to thin, and the executioner could return to his more private concerns.

He stayed up there long after the court undertaker had cut July down, until the warm summer darkness made further planning impossible. But by then he had everything doped out as far as it was possible to do that at this stage.

The position of the master bolt was no longer so worrisome, for he had bethought him that only the nearest trap to the ladder could be sprung with any real hope of beating Zeb's time. That meant he simply had to disconnect that trap from the other two, and rig its own makeshift bolt by the step-head. The court blacksmith could fix that in no time.

Of course, that lessening of ambition

also meant that there was no longer any question of besting Zeb twelve times over, as he had wistfully imagined. That side trap was made to take four at most; and a rough trial run, from ground level, timed with his stem-winder, had convinced him that when it got to actual performance he would never be able to handle more than three.

That enforced decision was a disappointment to him. But the chance of beating Zeb's time, and doing that with three subjects to his mere single — well, that chance seemed a great deal better than no chance at all.

There was a hell of a lot to be done before he would be ready to make the try; and certain rubs he could see in his way that were quite apart from the practical ones. But when at last he closed the gate of the gallows yard behind him, and set off across the square heading back to North Thirteenth Street, he did so with much more heart than when he had left there that morning.

It had been a rather better day too for Judge Parker.

Regarding the delayed Rainbird trial, The Reverend Mr Smythe had come from Tahlequah with his rail voucher earlier than he'd expected him. After giving the missionary a firm talking to in his chambers, he accompanied him downstairs to the courtroom where Prosecutor Clayton was waiting to take him through his evidence for a second time.

But the Presbyterian's continuing nice scruples, and Will Clayton's bumbling attempts to overcome them, had still not satisfied the jurist as being certain to send the young Cherokee to the gallows. Soon, in exasperation, he took over the cross-examination himself.

"Now then, Mr Smythe!" he began bodingly. "I wish to talk to you of blood, sir — *blood!* For the court knows full well, from other and later witnesses of the dreadful scene you were drawn to by the screams of the dying, that a very large amount of that fluid was bespattered around the room you were first to enter."

"Come now, man, it was coating the walls to wainscot height, was it not? Indeed, according to the submission of the Lighthorse policeman whom you found and beseeched to accompany you there, it had entirely discolored a once blue rug. There was even more of it on the ceiling in, ah, 'terrible swirls of color', according to my own note of that policeman's shocked and graphic words. *Blood, sir — blood!* And yet to hear you speak now of what you found, one would not suppose that the effect upon you had been lasting, Mr Smythe."

He paused and glowered down at the tense faced and shrinking missionary on the stand. "Of course the jury will understand that your work for many years among the Five Tribes has inured you to many harsh sights," he continued more softly. "They will realize that you would not react to the carnage you found in that room as they would surely react themselves with their gentler sensibilities." Here he bestowed a faintly sarcastic smile upon the stout Arkansan farmer who was the jury foreman, before returning his gaze to the delicate looking missionary.

"*Vengeance is mine saith the Lord — I will repay*," he quoted as his voice swelled back to its usual courtroom fullness. "But how can such repayment conceivably be made, gentlemen? Three innocent lives — innocent in every sense, for those poor ladies were emphatically *not* members of the sub-species that the prisoner was wont to consort with, by his own and his wife's admission. Indeed, at the time they were intent upon their sewing and, ahem, their other blameless domestic functions, when the fiend now before you broke in upon them inflamed with lust!"

Now his voice dropped down to a penetrating whisper. "Only think of the pity of it, gentlemen. Only think of their maidenly horror and alarms, their fervent pleas for mercy, their pathetic struggles . . . which only served to enrage this savage beast further, so that he had recourse to his knife . . . that appalling blade which, even when cleansed of all trace of the *red ocean* it had released in that once contented and happy homeplace, still retained the power to strike a chill into every heart in this courtroom when it was produced in evidence."

From the corner of his eye he observed that the farmer in the box was now surreptitiously wiping one of his cheeks. But some of the others still looked uncertain. Yes, it would need a shade more besides perhaps . . .

"Members of the jury, you are perhaps feeling a trifle hard done by to have such a case as this one to rule upon," he said kindly. "And in a practical sense you are unlucky, since had the prisoner confined his murderous and vile instincts to his own kind, the case would have been tried by an Indian court and not this one. However," he added distinctly, "as three blameless white ladies were his chosen victims, according to law it automatically becomes a matter for us to deal with here."

Then he repeated in the same near whisper: "*I will repay saith the Lord.* I am sure that such a small degree of repayment as is possible for such an outrage, in this lesser court than the one where the prisoner must shortly appear also, will echo that righteous and immortal message."

He then sat back, well satisfied, while J. Warren Reed rose with his thumbs in their usual position in his velvet waistcoat pockets, and did what he could to hold the defense case together. But he and Reed and Clayton, and all the other trained minds in the courtroom, knew now precisely where Calvin Rainbird would shortly be appearing; apart from the Greater Court that he had just mentioned.

★ ★ ★

The jury were not out for long before they filed back and confirmed that expert opinion.

Passing sentence then occupied another ten minutes of his time; which still left him with ample in which to get a meal at a Fourth Street restaurant nearby, in the congenial company of Will Clayton. Afterward he returned alone to the courthouse and worked on some papers until it was three o'clock. And then, of course, he broke off to watch the atonement of the man July from his usual vantage point in the bay window.

He had taken George Maledon's advice that July's didactic drawing power was sufficient for him to be hanged alone. Going by the size of the crowd in the stockade, that advice had been sound. He prayed earnestly for July's victim when it was over; then remained at his post overlooking the giant gallows for a few moments longer than his perceived duty required, puffing contemplatively on his pipe.

Isaac Parker often did contemplate the gallows in that private way. To him, it seemed to stand for all he had managed to achieve here, in the face of near-total lawlessness and barbarism. He was contemptuous of the growing number of its critics, and more resolved than ever to defend its certainties in what he saw as the chaotic flux and disintegration of modern life.

He was well aware that his foes in that holy struggle were to be found everywhere: in the Arkansas state legislative, in Congress, in the Supreme Court, and in the Democratic Party machine which combined its dislike of him personally, as an apostate to their cause, with its feeble-minded dislike of capital punishment. And of course there were many others besides. He had to be constantly on his guard lest the court should be undermined and destroyed.

So he often drew both strength and comfort just from looking at the symbol of his achievement. But never being a man to waste much of his precious time, he was about to turn away from the window and go back to his desk when a sudden movement outside caught his eye.

He gazed down again with a puzzled blink. For below, Maledon had just run nimbly up the gallows steps and was carrying out what looked like a strange kind of miming action, up on the platform. He blinked again; possibly the thick glass was distorting what he saw.

Of course, he knew that the court executioner was highly conscientious regarding his onerous duty, and now concluded vaguely that the fellow was probably checking the mechanism in some way. For while the judge was well aware of the gibbet's symbolical side, he was not mechanically minded in the least.

By thunder, how spry Maledon still was! he thought with a twinge of envy. He was ruefully aware that though he was the younger man by ten years, and had once been a fine athlete, it would now be quite beyond him to move that quickly. The penalty for sitting down so much all these years . . . And perhaps Maledon's having once been a soldier had helped to preserve him in later life . . .

With a sigh and a headshake he got back to his endless work again.

★ ★ ★

Despite the faint tinge of regret that comparison had left him with, when he walked home in the early evening he still felt that on the whole it had been a good day.

Part of his restless mind was already grappling with aspects of the morrow's trial — a bigamy case — but as he strode massively up Garrison Avenue, doffing his tall silk hat to the odd passing acquaintance, he was looking forward to this rare chance of spending a few hours with the family.

But that, alas, did not prove as enjoyable as he had anticipated (and for the usual reason that seemed to come up so often of late).

His elder son, Charles, had now left home for Saint Louis, but James was still with them. And, as he soon learned from Mary Parker, the boy stood in need of another so-called loan.

"Not again, surely!" he spoke out with marked dismay, as he lowered his great head wearily on the antimacassar. He and his wife had just finished their simple supper together and Peggy, the maid, was clearing it away.

"I am afraid so, dearest," Mary said plaintively once the door had closed. "I know it is not long since he — "

"Indeed it is not!" the judge snapped. "Does that youth think I am made of money? Does he suppose my masters in the Capital are prepared to supply this family with a cornucopia of funds? *Pah!* The truth is somewhat different — as you know only too well, my dear," he finished on a gentler and sadder note.

Mary Parker did know that. Although she was white haired and round faced and elderly looking, for well over a year now she had longed quite girlishly to buy one of the new hooped dresses; but the household budget could not stand that expense. Sometimes it did seem most unfair to her that Isaac's responsibilities should be so great, yet his rewards from the government so meagre. But she felt she must say what she could in defence of her erring youngest child.

"I know he is going through a rather — a rather distressing wild stage, dearest," she murmured hesitantly. "But I am persuaded it will not last."

"I am persuaded it *cannot* last," he retorted grimly. "I take it that he is not favoring us with his company on this occasion, but when he returns I shall make a point of — "

"I think he is, well, keeping out of the way, Isaac."

"As well he might! But I shall stay up to confront him nevertheless, however late his return, and I shall then pass sen-ahem. I shall make yet another attempt to induce that boy to face facts, Mary," he said crossly, and retired with an angry flourish to the pages of the *Elevator*.

5

THE confrontation with his son did not go well. James was both defiant and unrepentant, and (although he decided not to broaden his financial talk with the lad) he was almost sure that he smelt spirituous liquor upon his breath.

Introducing ardent spirits into the Indian Territories was an offence that unfailingly brought him to his highest pitch of rhetoric in the courtroom; so it was especially hard for him to ignore this sign of it within his own home. He went to bed a deeply troubled father.

A largely sleepless night did nothing to improve him next morning; and, after a silent breakfast in the company of the pale-faced miscreant, he set off morosely for the courthouse.

He did brighten a shade, though, when he saw that George Maledon was waiting for him on the corner with Garrison Avenue. It occurred to him that they had not walked to or from work together for some time.

Isaac Parker probably never realized that those occasional half mile walks he shared with his neighbor and associate were another of the sights of the town that had made it famous: along with the hangman's picture gallery; Mary Parker's forbidden but stubborn visits to the jail taking flowers and cookies for the condemned killers; and Maledon's own solitary walks to the scaffold when his rope — or ropes — were carried there from his workshop in a converted market bag, the nooses coiling down neatly outside from under its lid, with the eyes of thousands fixed upon them in fascination as he passed them by.

There was a similar curious effect when the huge and solemn figure of the judge strode along the city's sidewalks, with his small and apparently quite different companion trotting beside to keep up with him. It was a sight which always upset Mary Parker and Eunice Maledon about equally, for reasons which neither of them could altogether explain. But their menfolk found it quite natural to walk together in that way.

"Morning, Your Honor," Maledon called out as the jurist approached the corner he stood by. "Ain't this a fine mornin' still for early fall?"

"Indeed it is, Mr Maledon — I suppose," Parker said wanly as they fell in stride. The executioner tilted his thin bearded jaw at him as he caught that plumb miserable tone.

"You keepin' in good health, sir? Reason I ask, one a the baillies was sayin' to me only yestidee, he was sayin' how there's some flu strain about what makes you take it nigh as bad as the Injuns do."

"Indeed? No, I am not suffering the pangs of ill-health exactly. More the pangs of parenthood," he said with pursed lips.

"Oh. Oh that, sure. I guess I've had

a bait of that too, sir, since that girl a mine got to sparkin' age. You can't take your belt to 'em no more, which is above half the trouble I'd say."

"That may well be true. Though in our own case that is not — umm — precisely the problem, Maledon. But I confess that Mary and I are worried about James. We seem to be . . . losing contact with him in a way that causes us some distress, I must own."

The executioner was silent for the next half block, as they proceeded along the broad road. He set great store by his personal friendship with Fort Smith's leading citizen, and was usually careful to keep things strictly sociable when they walked together. He didn't want Parker to suspicion he was using the chance to make some pitch of his own, like other cityites were forever trying to do when they got close to him.

Now, though, he was in the kind of serious tight where he felt he had to take that risk. Although he was no hand with words (and specially not with Isaac's spade bit style of words), he tried hard to nudge their conversation where he wanted it to go.

"Puts me in mind of when Euny and I had that special bad time with our Annie, when she was goin' with that married bugger in — beggin' your pardon, sir — with that married man like up to Eureka Springs. Well, we did all we could to head her off him, but you know yourself what a horsing woman's like. Yeh, well, point I'm makin' is in the end I fixed to take my vacation all at once that year, if you recall, and we took the dratted girl down to the Gulf coast. And did that do the trick? — I'll say it did! After she'd sunned herself some, and got somethin' going down with one or two of them beach studs I shouldn't wonder, like I say she was in a way of bein' over the worst of it with him at Eureka Springs."

He paused and grimaced, running

out of steam before he had got to it properly. The judge gave him a puzzled sidewise frown.

"I guess what I mean to say, Your Honor, is there's nothin' as works like a vacation at these bad family times," he floundered.

"Ah. I follow you now. But I fear there is no question of my own family going on any such vacation," Parker said sadly. "For one thing, the present court schedule is far too congested for me to order such a lengthy recess as would be required. And for another, to be quite frank with you I could not at the moment afford it."

Maledon stared at him in astonishment. Like most of the servants of the federal court, he had always imagined that Parker lived on another financial level from theirs entirely. But he knew how straight he was in every way, and didn't doubt his word now. He was discouraged, but tried a final ploy.

"Is that a fact? Well I'll swan. And after all you done for 'em too, servin' the Almighty on the frontier line. Mind you, Your Honor, it wouldn't be needful to take Miz Parker and the servants along, would it? Just you and young Jimmy was more what I had in mind."

He tried to force a lyrical quality into his reedy tones. "Only dwell on how the two of you'd appreciate them glorious Californy redwoods come this time a year. Or back East e'en better. Fall in New England! Just the two a you there on your own like, mebbe fishin' some, breathin' that special air they got, and before you can say snap the difficulty atween you and Jimmy just ain't there no more and — "

"I fear not, Mr Maledon," the judge interrupted in a firm though friendly manner. "We went to see Charles in Saint Louis back in April, and even the most economical of breaks would be quite beyond me until next year, so straitened are my affairs. And as I mentioned, there is also the perpetual demands of the court. No, I am grateful for your well meant suggestion, but we will just have to work it out some other — by thunder, did you see that butterfly? — there, on the redbud in Mr Francis's garden! Ah, it is gone now . . . You know, I am almost certain it was a pale Milkweed — that is to say a female of the species. How extraordinary, to see one displaying so late! As you remarked at the outset of this most enjoyable stroll, we have been vouchsafed a truly most splendid late summer this year."

George Maledon ground his teeth in frustration as the pair of them neared the old stockade. He knew now for sure that he had to go at it some other way. For if the Old Man couldn't be got out of town for the record try, at the very leastest he had to be got out of his damned view window above the gibbet when he tried it. Elsewise he'd give Isaac a conniption fit for sure, and make just as sure that his own ass landed in the Ohio penitentiary, whether he'd beat Zeb's record or no.

He knew that being arm in armly with the Old Man like he was still wouldn't save his hide, did he give him a stunt so full of shameful levity as a speed hanging to look at.

* * *

Heck Anstey drove the tumbleweed prison wagon and its mule team down to the ferry slip by the Poteau River, with all the seventy-three thousand square miles of Indian Territory put thankfully at his burly back once more.

Flanking the Studebaker rig on each side rode Deputy Marshals Frank Pettigrew and Danny Olsen. Olsen's left arm was hunched in a dirty sling. Behind him trailed Anstey's big steeldust saddle mount. Tied to Pettigrew's mount was a pack horse with a slicker-covered body hitched over the saddle. The other pack animal sagged under the weight of a double load of those items of plunder which hadn't been squeezed below the prison wagon after they'd lost their young driver, back in the Plateau country on the north of the Choctaw Nation.

The rig itself contained nine equally battered and worn-down men in the cage section; a mixed bunch of Intruders, whiskey runners, whiskey cookers, thieves, woman killers, and one white counterfeiter whom they had picked up from the Indian Lighthorse police at McAlester. Each one shackled to a log-chained stanchion in the middle of the cage, as well as being confined by its strap-steel mesh. They sprawled on the hard benches on each side, looking dull-eyed across the thin strip of water at their final destination. Their usual stream of profanity had dwindled off to nothing now that they were so near to the Fort Smith courthouse.

The badge on Anstey's riding coat was old and chipped and tarnished. It bore an early number, showing that its wearer had been on the field force since the mid-Seventies when Parker first took over the federal court.

When Anstey had set out from the city three weeks before, he'd been aboard the steeldust, and young Jim Foreman had been up on the wagon seat where he was now. In a little while, as the senior deputy of the outfit, Heck would have to go and see the young driver's mother and tell her that he wouldn't be coming home. What he would take care *not* to tell her was how needlessly and lucklessly the kid had died; for Heck saw no sense in upsetting a widow woman who'd borne a passel of grief already on account of the government. For Billy Foreman, her husband, had also been swallowed up in the endless maw of policing the Territory.

But before that, he had to write out his report at the U.S. marshal's office (always a last straw task to an unlettered man like Heck) and then go see the court clerk to present the trip's expenses. None of the homecoming procedure was ever much to look forward to; but nevertheless he and the other two had begun to crave for it as their rough trip progressed and grew rougher.

It was just a hell of a hardluck note about the kid — the case of a stray bullet from a hysterical whiskey maker, who'd only fired in the air to hold them off while he scampered upstream to try and hide his coil and mash vat; which the smell would have taken them to whatever he'd done.

Only that slug hadn't just gone in the air where the moonshiner had intended. It had also gone through Jim Foreman's neck as he sat there on the seat holding in his mules.

"Where's that damn raft at?" Danny Olsen said through his teeth. Danny was a good-looking young fellow, but he didn't look good now. To Heck's experienced eyes he looked in a way of going gangrenous. They'd done what they could to burn that knife cut he'd taken from the wife beefer in the cage, but by the look of it the blade had been used to scrape chicken shit off of a perch.

"The buck's a-startin' to pole across to us now, Pettigrew murmured round his wad of chewing plug. "Appears like he's bringing some woman over in a buggy."

A short over-stressed laugh broke from Heck's thick lips. He grunted: "I don't know about you boys but I couldn't mo-lest as much as a june bug. So I reckon that's one as gets away from us. Her and a few more besides."

"Gwan, you'll be rearin' up on The Row with us fellers in no time, won't he Dan, uh?" Pettigrew said, signalling with his eyes over Olsen's slumped head that he was trying to gee him up over the last stretch home. Heck sent a return signal and forced a chuckle and said:

"Sure. It'll only take us a space of rest and no more trail grub to bring us round."

After the ferry had bumped on the

Territory side and the woman had tooled her light rig off the slip, Heck promptly drove the tumbleweed on to the square of planks. Just as promptly, the ferry dropped below its danger line; and more so when the three horses boarded. The negro with the pole said: "Oh-oh Mistuh Antsy suh, I doan know as she'll take the all of yuh in one trip. Das a big load a flesh you got in your cage suh."

"She better had hold up, John," Heck told him with a fatalistic shrug. "Since we ain't in no shape to go over in bits'n pieces. Not the way you mean it anyhow," he added thinly.

The raft surfaced with a sucking sound when he drove off it on the Arkansas side. A few minutes later he was heading the outfit up First Street. They passed by The Row in the totally disinterested frame of mind which was common to most members of the two-hundred-strong field force when they first returned from a spell of duty.

When the rig was parked in the federal wagonyard and they'd hitched the animals, the three of them limped into Marshal Hall's office. The marshal wasn't there at the time. There was just a job-waiting deputy in the outer office, reading a *Morrison's Series* with his haunch propped on the cool part of the centre stove. Heck said acidly: "Hate to disturb you, Art, but there's some unconvenient fresh prisoners outside. But go roust up a doc first because Dan here's took a bad cut."

Art Pellor began to say something sharp and brass-tipped in return. But then he took in the general look of Danny Olsen and he mumbled instead: "Sure, Heck, right. That new doc's on at the hospital and I should catch him there before he goes his round if I hustle. Meantime, d'you want a report sheet to write up on? There's a few there on the table."

Danny Olsen sat down slowly in one of the chairs by the table as Heck took the other one. Pettigrew coughed and said: "All right if I drift now, boss? Time I found out if I need to kick that drummer outen my bed again."

Heck Anstey knew that it wasn't really a joshing type situation about Frank Pettigrew and his wife's lasting salesman friend. But he chuckled as though it was a josh. "Sure. It only needs but one idiot to write up the nice time we had. Give my best to Sal."

When Art Pellor came back with a young doctor from the New Hospital, the medic looked inside Danny Olsen's sling and peeled his teeth momentarily off his lips. Then he said in a tone of careful blankness: "I've got a carriage out in the yard, Deputy. If you lean on me d'you think you can walk to it?"

"Well I just about reckon so," Danny said with a frail stopped-off giggle. "After these three weeks past, I reckon I do have about that much left in me, doc."

Heck gazed half-blindly at his sick partner's back, with the doctor's white-coated arm braced around it, as the pair went outside. And then his tired dancy mind veered ahead to the sweet caucus he'd be having presently with Jim Foreman's mother. Not to mention filling in every last lousy detail of the tumbleweed run on the form now in front of him. Sighing out a full breath, he reached for the pen propped in the inkwell and started in on *Day One* with his clumsy and slightly shaking fist.

But oddly enough, it was none of those three causes for despondency which got to him like the fourth one did.

★ ★ ★

"Oh — sorry, sir," he was saying about ninety minutes later. "I was lookin' for Mr Adams. I guess he must have switched his office, huh?"

"No, no, come right in, Deputy," Crawford Higgs said with a beckon. "Adams has now retired. I have been appointed in his place. Is that an expenses slip I see in your hand?"

89

The clerk of court waved the grizzled and blocky-looking lawman to a chair, and began studying the paper that was passed to him over the desk. His opaque brown eyes peered intently through the nose specs. Heck Anstey — an old hand at sensing trouble of any kind — felt his neck hairs on the raise.

"Let's see now," Higgs said in a tone which was now all business. "You've been out for three weeks with a stack of John Doe warrants in the Choctaw piece. Four of you — no, only three, according to this note here that you lost a man in the course of the duty. You should have entered it on the slip as three, Deputy."

"It was four for most all of the time," Heck said coldly. He sure as hell didn't cotton to those big blowed up eyes in the slimsy frames. They looked like they'd been coated with lick from a jar.

"Ah, that may be," the clerk said with a finger wag. "But, according to

Regulation Forty-seven, Section Six, of rules governing remuneration of federal funds to servants of district courts, any officer losing his life in court service shall be deemed as deceased from the time of his departure on the service concerned, rather than the — often hard to verify — date of his death." He smiled blandly at the battered and darkening visage of the longstanding field rider.

Heck Anstey looked back at this desk jockey, feeling too tired to get really mad at him. But he was already wondering how long that muted feeling would last. For the moment he let the quibble about Jim Foreman's living expenses go by. He waited cagily to see what else this bugger tried to finagle over the trip. For he was plumb sure now that was his game. It showed in every line of his pale and needlessly sweating phiz (unless finagling made you sweat — he wouldn't know).

"Now, as to the mileage money," Higgs continued. "The standard rate being six cents a mile, as you know, and I see here you've logged three hundred. Hm. That's a good round figure, Deputy." He flashed a nasty false smile, and tented his pale fingers reflectively on the desk.

"Of course, official estimates for rates of travel in the Indian lands vary considerably, as I have learned from a careful perusal of them before and since my arrival. But I must admit to a slight feeling of doubt, Anstey, when a mileage claim works out so neatly at a hundred a week. Have you any comment on that, please?"

By then Heck Anstey had a whole crowd of comments piled up at the back of his thick and leathery pillar of a throat; but for the moment they were gagging him. Higgs went on breezily: "Well, we'll come back to that in a moment. Now let's see — nine suspects captured, and no others recorded as dead. I must congratulate you there — most professional." He flashed that grin again. "Also, of course, no arrest payment is authorized in the case of dead outlaws. No doubt you are well aware of that fact," he added drily.

Heck finally found his voice, though it was thick with rage and incredulity.

"Mister, are you tryin' to say we keep 'em specially alive for a two-dollar scalp gain?"

"I suggested no such thing," the clerk said with another maddening wag of his forefinger at Heck's empurpled face. "The comment arose from the fact that I have studied records kept over a trial period regarding the condition of persons conveyed to this court for trial. In several such cases, it would seem that somewhat extreme — and some might say inhuman — efforts were made to keep prisoners extant, until at least the point where monies could be claimed upon them by their arresting officers. Now I make no accusation that is so as regards this trip of yours — though I see you make no specific mention as to the condition of your prisoners upon delivery at the jail."

"*God damn it, man!*" the old lawman finally thundered forth. "Are you sayin' as we'd ought to let 'em cash in in the cage so's the government can save a lousy two-buck a head on 'em? Mister Clerk, that ain't just what I swore on to do all those years ago!"

Crawford Higgs's brown orbs flicked for a second to Anstey's ancient badge. It didn't seem to give him any check whatever.

"Deputy, you are making far too much of a point which *I* made only in passing," he mouthed smoothly. "I am prepared — at least in this instance — to sanction the eighteen dollars you claim for bringing in your prisoners, without enquiring whether any of them are, in fact, near to death. But as I say, I am unhappy regarding the question of the mileage allowance. I must therefore ask you to supply verifying statements from each of your fellow officers on the trip as to the distance covered. And I would warn all three of you most seriously that it is an offence under

94

Section Five of — "

Heck Anstey was suddenly on his feet, with fury surging through his veins and all trace of his recent grief and exhaustion for the moment fled.

"Sonny you may not know it but you are in deep shit," he said softly, but with his dark-tanned cheeks pulled tightly into carved lines so that the scar on one of them writhed like a little white snake. "I'm seeing Parker about you, sonny, just as soon as my legs can take me there!" He wheeled and stomped out.

Crawford Higgs did not look at all discomposed by this information as he sat on at his desk. Instead, his lips formed a grin of quiet satisfaction.

6

JUDGE PARKER had been ensconced with a group of aldermen, in connection with the floatation of a civic bond involving government aid, when Anstey bulled into the presence of his personal clerk outside the door of his chambers.

By then the lawman's feelings had become so overheated that, in spite of the cool weather, he had tossed his coat on a chair and violently shoved up his shirt sleeves until they were half-tucked under the shoulder strips of his horsehide vest.

Heck Anstey's arms were covered in muscle and hard fat; and tattoos were crawling over them both. Altogether he made a fierce prospect as he planted them on his hips and demanded to see the judge pronto.

"Now you slack off, Heck," the

longstanding clerk said concernedly. "I know you're one of his First, but without you go in there a mite politer than how you are he'll soon set you back on your butt. And anyhow I won't let you, because he's in a huddle with some townsmen right now."

"More townsmen, huh?" Anstey muttered grimly. "There seem to be quite a few of those articles around here these days. How about after they're gone, Bobby?"

Bob Wilson hesitated. He knew that the boss had a tight schedule today, and that he planned to convene again downstairs once the deputation had left him. But he also knew that Heck Anstey could become a pretty tiresome visitor if he put off on him for long in his present mood.

"I guess I could slip you in right after the bigwigs are through. He'll kick my ass for it but what d'you care?" he complained grumpily.

"No he won't," Anstey prophesied as he slammed down into a chair. "When

I've said my piece he'll have sufficient ass to kick without needin' yours."

★ ★ ★

After he had been with Parker for some five minutes he wound up with some passion: Young Jim Foreman gave his life on that trip, Isaac. And Dan Olsen's in a way of givin' his too if I don't miss my guess. I went round to see that kid's mom right after I done wrote my report downstairs. And after I done told *her* I went to see this — this cityite fool who's tried to fill Charlie Adams's job. Like I say, he's the kind as would skin a louse for the hide and tallow. It just ain't good enough after what we all went through on that damn run. Now it's a hell of a long space since I first said *I do* to you in this building, and I never called you oncet until now. But now I am callin' you. I want that stupid clerk fired off the job — or you can take this . . . " And then he disgustedly slapped a palm at the badge on his vest.

Judge Parker met his hot gaze steadily with the famous icy blue stare. "There is no need for profanity, Anstey."

"There is though!" Heck blustered. But by now, as Bob Wilson outside had told him would happen, he felt the Old Man's authority pressing down on him. He had a certain way of making that happen which couldn't be understood, only felt.

"I didn't mean to talk profane to you, sir. But as for that idiot, that Higgs, I claim it's a sorry thing I've had to fight for pennies with one like him right after having run-ins with Territory outlaws for most of these past three weeks!"

"Yes, I can see that was rather trying for you," Parker replied stiffly. "But the clerk of court — any clerk of court — is perfectly right to exercise discretion and vigilance as to the disposal of funds he is entrusted with."

He came to his feet and stepped around the desk to tower over the large field rider.

"I appreciate that you are presently overwrought, and perhaps not quite aware of what you have just asked me to do for you. In any event I cannot do it. Mr Higgs was appointed by our masters in the Capital, not by me. I have no powers to reverse his appointment. As for your, ahem, ultimatum concerning the surrender of your symbol of office, that decision must of course rest with you alone."

He paused for a moment, then went on more kindly: "Be sensible, man. Pesky clerks come and go. But you and I have gone on together for some fifteen years, Heck. Fifteen years in which, between us, we have consigned many a heinous wretch to the judgement of the Almighty — to say naught of all the lesser although still vile criminals whom you have also apprehended over that period. Take my advice — don't throw that fine record away in a fit of pique over a mere clerk's excessive zeal for his humble task."

He peered at the sullen deputy, with the penetrating gaze of one who was accustomed to divining much from shifting shades across the human countenance. His tone altered subtly. "And to be practical about it, while I should naturally furnish you with my recommendation for any future employer, facts dictate, alas, that in view of your mature years such an employer would probably be — "

"Some prairie town wantin' a prairie sheriff," Anstey cut in bitterly. He still felt very sore.

"Well, I would certainly try to do better than that for you," Parker said with a sudden smile of genuine warmth and friendship. "But pray think it over hard before you take such a drastic step. Believe me, I know how thankless a duty it can be to labor in the Lord's vineyard here on the edge of civilization. I have many, many times felt much as I think you now feel. So you must consider at length, Anstey — and I need hardly say how much I hope you will heed my words."

His remarkable memory then dredged up a detail from this officer's file. He swiftly bent it to his purpose. "You like to bet, I believe. Betting takes money — as well you must know."

Heck chewed at his bottom lip in frustration. He might have known it would end in being turned around his thumb in this usual half-kicked, half-gentled, know-all fashion. Hadn't it always been so, howsomever he'd got gunned or knifed or generally stomped on in between spells of listening to his medicine tongue?

But mad as he still was all through, it came to him that if he'd stood fifteen years of such treatment from the scum of the Nations, then maybe it was dumb to kite up in the air over one pen-shover.

"I'll think it over all right," he mumbled ungraciously as he touched his hatbrim and left. But the judge smiled broadly to himself after he was alone.

The confident smile did not remain on his face for long. Instead it became thoughtful and puzzled. He was now recalling his own brief exchange with Crawford Higgs, when the officious new clerk had even had the temerity to question his order to issue a rail voucher to a witness.

Perhaps, as he had put it to the irate deputy, Higgs was just showing understandable zealousness in his fresh appointment . . . But as he shrugged into his robe and went downstairs, there was a nagging unease in his mind that proved hard to banish and replace with details of the complex postal fraud that awaited his attention.

★ ★ ★

"Ah, Mr Maledon, just the person I'm looking for!" Crawford Higgs called out cheerily as he all but bumped into the hangman on the courthouse porch, two days later.

"Is that a fact?" he grunted sourly as he stood aside for the clerk to go on by. He took hold of his pipe by the clay bowl, and removed it to hawk a brown spindrift near the clerk's well-shone shoes. But they had come to a resolute halt beside him.

"I wonder if I might have a word with you in my office?" Higgs said with a blank chummy beam.

"I'm too busy right now," he told him bluntly. "Got to check my hangin' book with the top office. I ain't got time to — "

"This will take very little of your time — Deputy," Higgs murmured, with a push on that last common word which made the Prince of Hangmen flush under his beard. It graveled him that his official station had never been raised up to fit with his nationwide rep; and even more so that a mere clerk should remind him of that.

"If it's about my split with the

undertaker again, I ain't got no more to say to you on that matter," he growled as he followed Higgs inside and then down the hall to his office. "Hundred a head is our duly authorized rate, and I don't aim to tell you over how we cut it atween us or how we put in for it. If you can't foller that it ain't my fault."

"No, it isn't about that — not for the moment anyway," Higgs said, as he made a half-bowing and heel-clicking grandstand of opening the door for him. "Go right in and be seated, Deputy."

"No," he continued in the same mocking manner as he slid into his own chair. "This time it's your rope I wanted to discuss."

"What about my rope?" George Maledon demanded. He removed the pipe again to utter a short cackle of derision. "Since when does a feller in your line know aught about rope?" he asked with withering sarcasm.

"Not much, I grant you," Higgs

owned smoothly. He tipped backward and pulled out a drawer and groped within it. "When I said *rope*, I meant more precisely your habit of buying it a long distance — a costly long distance — away from Fort Smith. And then there is the additional cost of the rope itself. I have looked into that. Your rope would seem to come more expensive by far than rope of a similar kind that could be obtained elsewhere — and much nearer."

He took his hand from the drawer and tossed a thick rubber-banded roll of receipts in front of the glowering executioner.

"These are your bills from the Saint Louis supply house which — so you claim — is the source of all your various consignments purchased over the years in order for you to perform your court duties."

"*And so it goddam is!*" he was informed, on an outraged rising screech. "Reason I go all the ways to Saint Lou for it is I need the best cord that's goin' for my machine! That Saint Lou house *is* the goddam best — elsewise they wouldn't have the custom of the Prince a Hangmen! What I guess you've costed it against, Mister Clerk, in your amacher fashion, is *cheap sisal. I don't use cheap sisal in my work!*"

Crawford Higgs waited patiently until the spitting and turkey-gobbling of his visitor had at last subsided for lack of breath. Then he leaned forward and raised his own voice for the first time.

"All from Saint Louis, you claim? Then how come those advertisements I used to see back in Ohio? The ones that featured the slogan: *If it's strong enough for Maledon then it's strong enough for you?*"

The clerk's smile had now taken on a predatory sawtoothed edge. "I don't recall it was a Saint Louis company that boosted itself with that slogan. It was a company based elsewhere, wasn't it, Mr Maledon? I await your comments."

"You're about to get them too," he told him with a matching cagey grin of his own. "That was just a helpin' hand I gave to some young fellers in Chicago who were just startin' out in business, like to encourage 'em as I hoped in the common interest of producin' better cord. Like I allus say, what's in a name? I was proud to let them deservin' young fellers use mine iffen they chose to. But that don't mean I ever used their rawhide product! I wouldn't use that Chicago cord to string up a banty rooster," he finished with total sincerity.

"*Gave*, Mr Maledon? *Gave?*" Higgs repeated harshly. "Don't you mean *sold*? Don't you mean you traded your government appointment totally illegally, in order to feather your own nest?"

George Maledon abruptly stood up and kicked the chair away. "Are you fixin' to prove that, Mister Clerk?" he jeered reedily. "You'll waste a sight of time if you are. I ain't some Old State pilgrim like them you kicked around in Ohio I shouldn't wonder. You'll find the difference if you get crosswise of *me!*"

Crawford Higgs eyed him coolly and thoughtfully for a moment. "I believe you," he said then. "I believe exploring that particular avenue would prove — unprofitable."

"No shit," said George Maledon, hawking at the office floor.

" — but I still have no intention of allowing further expenditure on these extravagant steamboat trips of yours to Saint Louis," the clerk pursued-doggedly. "If you have to go up there to check each consignment before delivery — which, no doubt, you would insist was needful if I queried that — there is no reason on Earth why you shouldn't travel the more economical way by rail."

Maledon eyed him more balefully still. There *was* a reason why he chose to take his annual trips to Saint Lou by boat; though it had nothing to do with the rope-buying. It had everything to do with the wild and prolonged red light sprees he liked to indulge in, up and down the riverside whorehouses, before and after concluding his transaction at the rope suppliers.

He began to spin a yarn in his mind for this feist-like clerk, to the effect that the river trips were vital to keep the rope damp and supple; but in the end he didn't bother to bullshit him over that. By then he'd made a decision that he couldn't abide Crawford Higgs for any longer, and that he didn't intend to try to.

So all he said to him finally was a venomous: "You'll be hearin' some more about this, Mister Clerk."

And then, for the second time after an angry officer of the court had just stormed away from his presence, Crawford Higgs stretched back comfortably in his chair with a Cheshire cat grin.

7

H E caught the judge in his chambers during the noon adjournment; after having a slight dispute outside them with the overly protective Bob Wilson.

By then, the Prince of Hangmen wasn't in a tolerant mood toward awkward clerks of any kind; even the more harmless Arkansas-born tribe like Bob's. "I don't care if he's talkin' to Saint Francis of asses his own self," he hissed at him, with a dig of his horny thumb at the clerk's blue-suited stomach. "You go in there *right now* and tell him I've got to see him."

"Gee-rusalem, George, how can I?" Bob protested. "He's trying to squeeze a railroad man to up the reward for that safe car that got blown last month on the Katy. There's just no way I can . . . "

But then he felt Maledon's paw drop on his shoulder, and made the mistake of looking directly into the hangman's eyes.

That was a combination of pressure which often worked wonders for him; even with law-abiding desk jumpers like Wilson here, who weren't apt to come his way professionally in a million years. He knew just how it worked on them too: they fell to wondering what his touch would seem like if it was near about their last living sensation; and what his eyes would also seem like if they were the last set you ever looked back at. He could tell all that easy enough, on his end.

The trick didn't always push difficulties over for him; but it did that now with Robert Wilson.

"So all right all *right!*" he snapped, jerking spasmodically away and heading for the inner door. "I'm gettin' tired of this job, I really am! What with having you come latherin' after him, and that old deppity with the tattoos the other day just as ringy, I'm applying for a transfer, that's what I'll do! If that new man's crazy enough to switch from Ohio down here, whyinhell shouldn't I switch from here up to a decent civilized place like Ohio? These lousy golblasted boondocks jam full of killers with or without stars on — *I'm right sick of it!*"

But then he promptly simmered down and tapped quietly on the door and chinked it open, giving a clerkish cough.

"Sorry to intrude, Judge. But I've got the court executioner here and he's wishful to see you pretty urgent."

Isaac Parker looked irritably over the head of the railroad official who was with him. But he wasn't really vexed to be interrupted, since the talk with him was getting nowhere due to his obstinate stone-walling.

"Ahem, Mr Watson," he said, rising. "You must forgive me but it would seem I have another visitor. Kindly inform your board and president that, in my opinion, we will not succeed in apprehending the Bill Cook gang without a much more substantial inducement from yourselves. Good day to you, sir."

"What is the meaning of this, Maledon?" he said crossly when the train man's replacement stood before him. "I am due downstairs directly, and I cannot — "

"It's about the new court clerk," he was told in reedy quivering accents. *"Iffen he don't go then I do!"*

Parker opened his mouth to utter a chilly reproof; but then he slowly closed it, and stroked his chin beard in a reflective way for a good two minutes. "Explain precisely what lies behind that extraordinary remark," he then commanded.

After George Maledon had given him at least three rambling, and mostly shouted, accounts of his dealings with Crawford Higgs, the judge waved him to be silent. After a further period of frowning consideration he said: "I really must go now. I wonder, Mr Maledon, if you could arrange to stay on at the courthouse until we stop tonight? In the circumstances I will make that as early as possible. I think we should discuss this matter at some length."

A brief look was then exchanged between the pair of them which was quite different in character from the way that either looked at anyone else.

"Sure, Your Honor, I'll wait on you until the recess," George Maledon mumbled contentedly. "Shall we talk up here again?"

"No, I think not. Wait in the porch, if you will. We can walk home together — that will be more private."

★ ★ ★

The hangman heard the gavel go down at around a quarter of eleven. But after the people in the courtroom had all spilled out past him there was still no sign of the judge. He sat patiently on the end of one of the long benches that lined the equally long porch, which extended the entire frontage of the building.

At last Parker came hastening out through the double doors.

"I am so sorry to have kept you, Maledon. There was some confusion over one of the briefs for tomorrow, which I had to settle." He finished buttoning his top coat and donned his tall hat. "Well, let us be off then."

There was a strong taint of ozone on the still night air outside. Maledon took a testing sniff at it as they began to cross the square to the stockade gate. "Feels about to storm, Your Honor."

"Yes — how annoying! I do not wish to be distracted by the elements from what needs to be said between us."

That imperious wish proved vain; for thunder rolled and large dime-sized drops suddenly battered the top of his hat when they were nearly at the gate. His companion touched his arm. "Better get under the gibbet roof for a space, sir, till it's passed over. That's our closest cover from here, and I know better'n most it don't let in the wet."

Isaac Parker allowed himself to be led reluctantly toward the small gallows yard on the north side of the square, which was almost filled by the looming contraption its low square fence surrounded. Maledon clicked open the entrance gate, and the two of them hurried, head-down, along the short flagstone path between the patches of green lawn on each side.

Despite the continuing heavy rain, Parker stopped slightly short of the great hanging machine and looked up at it. Little of its outline was visible in the teeming dark, but he stood there for about a half-minute with the rain pouring off him. Lightning cracked, and illumined his large black figure. George Maledon, by now sheltered under cover, felt an odd tremor pass through his body which had nothing to do with the walls of water all around him.

It came to him that, as far as he knew, until now the Old Man never had gone near the gibbet that he sent so many others to. And now that he had, somehow it gave off a spooky effect.

Then he seemed to snap to again and came on under cover. He said wryly: "This was supposed to be a *private* conversation, Mr Maledon."

His workaday friend was confused by that remark. "Couldn't be much more private than here, Your Honor."

The judge sighed. "Perhaps you are right . . . do you have any tobacco with you by some chance? I have foolishly left my own supply upstairs when I changed."

"Sure, sir, hep yourself. But it's only common Durham, mind."

"Blackwell's Durham is much under-rated. I frequently smoked it myself when I was a young man in Mirrouri." He paused, and tilted his head upward at the boards of the gallows platform. " . . . before my life led me where it has, and before President Grant persuaded me to become the, ahem, Hanging Judge."

"Is that a fact, sir? Gen'ral Grant — gaw bless him — knowed a good man when he saw one I'm thinking."

Parker sighed again, and George Maledon perceived that the weather must have dampened his spirits some. He recharged his own pipe bowl from the returned sack. The two of them lii up together from the judge's match and leaned back on two inner sides of one of the fat corner balks. High above them, the rain pounded on the sloping canopy which covered the gallows, then spattered into a twenty-foot long shallow earthy trench near their feet.

Maledon said sociably: "Duty bailie's puttin' out the courtroom lamps, sir. I make it you don't stay behind to see that done most nights."

"No, indeed. It must be quite an arduous task, especially for a small man like McConnell there. I had no idea it required the use of a ladder — but of course it does. Those sconces are set quite high."

They both puffed away, looking through the rain and the streaky courtroom windows on that side, where the bailiff was shifting his step-ladder from lamp to lamp along the inside walls. When the last one had blinked out, the only two small points of light left in the total blackness came from the pipes of Judge Parker and George Maledon.

The symbolism of that was not lost upon the jurist; and it served to concentrate his mind upon the purpose of this meeting. He tentatively began to approach that purpose.

"You know, it is rather odd that you should have brought to my attention this impasse you reached with the court clerk. Because only a short time ago I received a similar complaint from one of the field force."

The hangman sucked expressively on his stem. "There ain't nothin' so mortal strange about that, Your Honor. Seeing that man Higgs, he's done upset most everyone who works for the court by now."

"Has he indeed," the judge murmured. "I suspected that might be the case."

He hesitated, seeking for a form of words that would not commit him; then shrugged that cowardly instinct impatiently away. He reminded himself that he was not now bandying words with his own kind at the Fort Smith bar; he was with a simple man who would understand only simple plain dealing.

"I think this fellow Higgs may have been sent here by our enemies, Maledon. There is a certain assistant attorney general whom I know to be one of those enemies — indeed, one of the most unprincipled. That person wields considerable influence with the Ohio people. When Adams retired I did not expect his post to be filled from Ohio — and I also did not expect it to be filled by someone as patently unsuited to our ways as this Higgs!"

he finished forcefully.

The hangman nodded, and spat into the rain. "Yeh that makes sense, Your Honor. I'm thinking them dehorns in Washin'ton have gone and sicked us with an anti-hangin' spy."

"Well, yes, in essence I fear that may be true. And I think I can apprehend their strategy — that is to say, their plan of campaign, Maledon. No one knows better than they do how little money I am allotted with which to pay the court staff. Why, take only Mr McConnell whom we were just discussing. McConnell is an excellent bailiff — yet I know he must make ends meet with various farming activities which often make him late, or exhausted, for his duties here. Just as, no doubt, his court work makes him overdue with his sowing, or planting, or whatever. And as you will know, many of the deputies who work so hard and valiantly in the Territory are also employed part-time. It is plainly most unsatisfactory. Yet despite my many pleas for sensible funding, made ever since I became the presiding judge here, that has steadfastly been refused me!"

Realizing that he had lapsed into a speech, he tried his best to continue without further undue rhetoric.

"As you must know, the perfectly right and just decisions of this court are now forever being challenged by Congress and the Supreme Court. That is still the main weapon that is being used against us. But now I fancy there is another besides: the use of an *agent provacateur* — umm, a trouble maker — sent to promote disharmony and resignations among the poorly paid folk who form the bulk of our work force."

"If that scheme succeeded, it would make it that much more plausible to accuse us of running the kind of backward and inefficient system of justice here which is their basic contention — and thus that much easier to destroy us."

He felt he had still tended to be

over-fulsome, and added in a none too hopeful tone: "Do you understand all this, Mr Maledon?"

In actual fact the executioner had quickly grasped the nub of the matter for himself, without having to pay much mind to Isaac's standard roundaboutation. "Sure," he grunted. "The thing is what to do about it, uh?"

"Yes," Isaac Parker said gratefully. "That is *precisely* the, ahem, thing."

"You couldn't just tell the eastern bosses he's turned out a poor hand at frontier law-keepin', and get 'em to take him off of our backs that away?"

Alas, no. His appointment is quite outside my control. And his actual work is unexceptionable — I mean it is good enough."

Maledon tapped out some dottle on the gallows post, snarling quietly to himself as he did so. He cast a measuring glance at Parker's indistinct worried face. "Then I'd say there's onliest one way to handle it, sir. I might just have an idee on that. But

I ain't none too sure you'd much admire it."

"No," the judge mused thoughtfully. "I suppose I might not. But then again, you know, we lawyers are very used to not ascertaining entirely what are the facts of the matters requiring our attention."

"You mean you'd just as soon not know, uh?" he was asked bluntly.

Judge Parker felt most uncomfortable; yet he was resolved to complete this awkward discussion. He knew how resourceful and capable his henchman could be, for he had proved that to him before now. And he shared his evident belief that the problem could not be solved in a wholly open manner.

"Perhaps you could give me just a *slight hint* of what is in your mind. My own might then be easier," he said cautiously.

George Maledon took the point. "Yeh, sure, you'd like a glimmer to go by. Well sir, that clerk's got hisself a pert little wife, you know. One a them fractious southron women, only more so. They've got theirselves a nice home on Fourth, one a them nice new cottages on them fresh-sold lots there."

"And?" the judge prodded.

The hangman now chose his own plain words with some care. He grasped how much the Old Man wanted to know — and what he surely didn't want to know.

"The news goin' round town is them two spat back an' forth a good deal, sir. Anyhow that's how Eunice heard it by the backfence telegraph, the way that women do. Seems like the clerk, he may appreciate his home cooking an' all, but other ways he don't go home for it altogether so much."

The judge swallowed rather noisily beside him. But maybe he was only clearing his throat, for the next thing he said was a loud: "I do believe the rain is finally subsiding, Mr Maledon. Perhaps we can now venture forth."

On the way home they spoke mainly of other things.

8

THERE was nobody down in his book for the next morning; and, with the judge's sanction, he skipped his alternative jail chore and took himself off to pay a couple of calls in the town.

The first of those calls was upon Hal Rathbone at Sixth Street. He picked up a fresh batch of likenesses which the photographer had waiting for him, and talked with Hal for a spell in back. Then he went on to the corner of Garrison and First and turned down the hill toward the waterfront.

His progress slowed as he came to the line of tall parlor houses, in the lower section of First Street that was known as The Row. Like many a visitor to that part of town, he loitered outside, uncertain as to which establishment would receive his patronage.

One difference, though, was the expression on the hangman's whiskery countenance: it was far more baleful and malevolent, and far shorter on erotic expectation, than the expressions of most men who visited The Row.

That had not always been the case. In times gone by, his post-hanging orgies there had been notorious. But then Judge Parker had stepped in and given him a stern lecture as to the scandalous effect of such sprees on the standing of the Fort Smith court. In that as in most other aspects of his life he was totally subservient to the judge, and from the time of that talking-to his red light capers had been conducted well away from the city limits.

So his present indecision had nothing to do with that. As his gaze roved over the gaudy shingles beside each house, he was simply assessing his present relationship with the particular businesswoman who ran each place, and her individual trustworthiness or lack of it. (And also her fear of him or lack of that.)

To take them in line, first there was Mrs Brigid Gallagher, the boss of the House of Eiran; next door came Miss Rosa Lou of The Riverboat House; then Young Mrs Seymour, third generation of the ex-sodbuster family who ran the fancily named Madame June's Salon; Miss Elsie Randall of Hook-and-ladder Kate's; Mrs Aaron P. Wodis of The Venus Rooms; Mrs Latimer of Wild Rose; Mrs Jones of South Seas Magic; Miss Buttle of Sal and Francie's; and, on the other end, Mrs Jones's other segundo-run place, Touch of the Orient.

. . . The trouble with most all of them was they'd talk. The old josh about nothing spreading like a secret among women was increased about a thousand per cent when you applied it to parlor house women. And most of them were too rich by far for him to try buying their silence, even if he was dumb enough to try that. Why, he reckoned they could forget all about taxes for the whole US of A, if the boss women in that single rawhide block there could be made to shoulder the burden instead . . . "

Of course, the one who he'd always gotten along with worse than any of them was Rosa Lou. Back in the days when he was a steady customer, the proprietress of The Riverboat House had annoyed him plenty, with her so-called sense of humor. She'd done funny things like tucking him in one of her beds when he was full of panther juice, along with an article who'd looked like his grandmother when he woke up in the morning. Funny stuff like that. And he had no reason to think she'd changed any since those bygone times when she thought she was so cute and smart . . .

But he had to own that the damned woman did know everything to do with her business; and most things to do with all her opposition's business, come to that. He reluctantly decided that he had to go talk to her; which might lead on to mean he had to cut her into it as well; but he was not yet resigned to doing that. He felt it would be almost less painful for him to send money to an anti-hanging fund than to present it — for no poon whatever — to The Riverboat House.

He clumped up the steps there and pounded on the door with its steamboat-shaped brass knocker. A moment later one of Rosa Lou's primly dressed maids opened up, with a rustle of starched linen.

"Come right in, sir," she mouthed mechanically. "If you'll take the first right and just wait a space, then in a moment — "

"No, honey, I won't take first right. Go tell the boss I'm here. Say it's George Maledon."

The maid hadn't been on the team when he was last here. But of course she knew the name. Her eyes went wide and she backed away fast. He sat down and waited on one of the

131

madam's bitsy gold hall chairs, using the time to leaf critically through his latest photos for the Collection.

Miss Rosa Lou was at her most syrupy sarcastic when she came through to him.

"Mr Maledon! — this *is* a surprise! How long has it been, now? My, my, must be all of five years! Of course, you must be a sight older now — that's obvious when I look at you. I guess that's the reason for it. But even so, five years is a long time to lose touch with an old friend . . . "

He levelled a horny finger at her greeny glinting eyes. "You hobble your lip, sweetheart. An' you don't look so hot yourself nowatimes, come to that."

But he was grudgingly aware that wasn't true. The famous bosom was still its incredible unsagging self within the skimpy confines of a yellow top-dollar Worth gown; the waist below it was still cinched into a space a man's hands could go round and still manage to divide his fingers on the other side; and her towering heap of cornsilk hair above hadn't one white hair in it yet. Her face was still flawless (save for those evil eyes). Her legs had always been her one weakness — they were stumpy before and they were now stumpier yet. He growled gratefully: "You ain't ailin' too bad from your gout I hope, sweetheart . . . "

"How kind of you to be concerned," Miss Rosa said more harshly. "Might I enquire to what I owe the pleasure of this meeting?"

"Well it ain't noways what you figure, that's for sure."

"Oh, but I *don't*, Mr Maledon. Oh no — not any more, that's very plain."

He scrabbled angrily in his beard. "Will you kindly get off my case, woman? I've got somethin' to put to you."

"Really? That's the very thing I doubted, Mr Maledon. But do go ahead if you can.

"Just shut up and listen," he grunted. "Have you had any new court custom passin' through in the last few weeks?"

Rosa took another of the little chairs, with a courtesan's instinctive leg show which made the executioner groan and roll up his eyes. "Just answer the question, will you?"

"Sure I will. I don't aim to cause you any wistful memories, Maledon. So I'll just answer the question. Do you mean new bailiffs and deputies and suchlike? I guess there may have been. But none that I'm specially aware of."

"I mean clerks. And one consarn clerk in perticklar. A ranahan with nose glasses pinched over a set of eyes like brown marbles. And glued down yeller hair, and a way of sweatin' like a blown horse all the time for no reason."

"Oh. Oh yes, you must be speaking of our Mr Higgs, Maledon. He splits his custom between ourselves and Mrs Wodis." Her handsome features grew slightly complacent. "I guess he knows our two places are the class of what's available in this town. Mr Higgs strikes me as a gent of some discernment."

"Does he now . . . " But his thoughts were already drifting off the immediate conversation, as he tried to make himself decide in favour of doing business with the Wodis woman rather than with his old enemy here.

He nibbled at his moustache ends in frustration. He was recollecting how the Wodis woman had always tried to set herself above him. He still had a sore memory of when she'd had his sodden carcass pitched into the street once in the old days. And he mustn't overlook she had some hightone connections, too. He'd threatened to land the judge on her after that time, and she'd just laughed in his face and bade him to go ahead. Very likely she'd got one or more of Isaac's dinner company on her string, and knew she'd manage to stay in business howsoever he badmouthed her to the Old Man.

. . . So it looked as if he had to choose this green-eyed bitch here. That piece of knowledge stuck in his craw like a maggot-riddled biscuit. If it wasn't for the fact he'd seen a personal angle in going through with it, aside from aiding Parker, he would have got up and left at that crucial moment of decision.

He forced out: "There's certain people — certain bigwigs in high up circles — as nacherally don't concern them as ain't no better'n they should be like yourself — these people want that clerk taken down a peg or two."

Observing that the madam's face was hardening over that approach, he strove to make his discourse a shade more palatable to her. But his old habits died hard where she was concerned.

"The thing is, Rosa, they're ready to pay a bit to do it, too. Now for oncet in your fallen life answer me straight: are you willin' to help me get the deadwood on this Higgs?"

. . . He could read her greedy mind close enough. Sharing that cheap clerk with the Wodis woman wasn't apt to be giving her much of a skim off him. Yep, she'd come round to doing it all right; but he didn't relish the business discussion that lay ahead. He'd got the Old Man to divvy up a stake to do this with, but it wasn't enough alone to buy over a prosperous Row madam with. He'd need to lean on her as well, that was for sure . . .

Rosa Lou tapped one of her gold spool heels thoughtfully on the polished floor. "What exactly did you have in mind?"

He told her what he had in mind; including the double cinch he intended to use on Crawford Higgs, in case one wasn't sufficient. She heard him out in poker-faced silence. Then:

"What's my slice to be if I went along with this shenanigan? — and don't waste both our time trying to chisel on it like you always did in this house."

He bared his teeth but let that shaft go by him. "Hundred and twenty, take it or shake it. I ain't authoritized to go above that, honest to God."

Rosa Lou uttered a short burst of meaningless commercial mirth. "You figure — you seriously figure, Maledon — that I'd go to all that inconvenience, and lose a steady customer too, for a picayune one-twenty?"

"Tell you the truth I wouldn't." He paused and added in no special tone: "But the judge comes into the deal too, Rosa."

"With *you* cut in I'd a fair notion who'd shuffled," she retorted drily. "And you don't need to give me all the rest of that old pitch — how he'd close me down and run me out and how you'd half-strangle me to remember you by! I've heard it all before, Maledon!"

"Mebbe you have. That don't mean all of them things wouldn't happen." He looked suddenly into her paint-ringed eyes the way he knew how to. "Make no mistake of that."

As he spoke, he slightly tilted the

bunch of unwrapped daguerreotypes in his hands; so that Rosa Lou found herself looking at the one on the top, which was a rather frightening record of the depraved and defiant features of Calvin Rainbird.

Her self-confidence took a marked dip. "Sure I know that," she murmured quietly. "For Christ's sake keep your creepshow pictures to yourself."

Her tone became more wheedling. "But you must know it really ain't enough for it. What you call your double cinch is apt to tie up two of my rooms!" Her indignation returned in full measure with that thought. "You could always go and try your luck with that la-di-da Wodis bitch! See what *she* makes of your proposal for a fast one-twenty! *Hah*!"

He decided it was time to put up the figure he'd had in mind all along for the woman side of it. "I'll raise to one-fifty. Honest to God I can't go higher or I would."

Rosa Lou tapped her heel again.

She was versed in the ways — and the lies — of men, and she didn't think this one was lying now. She could see this was important to him; and, by extension, to the all-powerful shadow of Parker which as always stood beside him.

That combination wasn't a thing which anyone in Fort Smith would lightly buck, whatever their side of the tracks. It was true that The Row lay outside the court's reach. But she didn't plan to risk her whole future on a legal technicality like that.

Also, though she had not deemed it advantageous to mention it, Crawford Higgs wasn't a client that she set much store by. He was the kind that liked them very young; but needed them to be pretty old to handle his specialist capers. She knew that sooner rather than later he would have become an unprofitable nuisance. So one-fifty on him, right now in her hand, was a better offer than the executioner appreciated.

"All right, I'll go along for that — in here right now."

After he'd given it over he grunted: "Does Higgs come night-times or any old time?"

"Always in the early evenin', so far. After he quits his work, I guess. He has a regular date with us Wednesdays. Saturdays, he goes to the Venus." She slightly pursed her bright lips. "You could say he's a person of fixed habits."

He studied a moment with snarling concentration, tugging at his beard.

"Right, woman, so this is what I want you to do . . . "

★ ★ ★

On the following Wednesday, after seeing to a twosome in the afternoon, George Maledon was drinking with a few lingering tourists in a colored bar on the waterfront. They were asking him the usual dumb questions.

"How do they act when you tie their

legs together? Do they shake so much they stomp on the trap-floor? Why don't you cut them down after it so they don't dangle there looking so sad? Do they have to have them blinders on by law? Don't you feel funny to have their kin up there behind you on the bench while you're doing it? Has anyone ever thrown down on you or pulled a knife?"

All manner of stuff like that which he'd answered a hundred times before. Today he paid less mind to it than usual, his ears cocked all the while for sounds more distant than the yokels' stupid drunken voices.

"My, my, seems I've gone empty," he mumbled, holding up his stein with an elaborate air of surprise. An obliging yokel took it from him, and staggered off to get it filled again.

As he quaffed steadily at the refill, weary to death of their questions, he began to drone out the comprehensive and pseudo-genial spiel he always kept ready in his mind for such brainless groups. By now he had it off by heart. It was a sight less irritating than answering their questions.

"The thing about my trade, boys, is you need strong wrists for it. That's why I make a point of keepin' Mrs M well provided for in the cordwood department. Heh-heh! Yes sir, twicet a week at the leastest I'll be out there in my woodlot swinging my good ol' ten pounder. Folks like you who're only in town now and then for the hangin's, you might look over my fence and say to yourselfs: *There's a feller who believes in lookin' ahead more'n most do to next winter-time*. Heh-heh! Well a course, that's true enough in a sense. Like I say, Mrs M appreciates the result of all my choppin'. Heh-heh! But what I do it for acksherly is to keep my wrists in shape for my job. Why, I do b'lieve my ol' German pot has gone down again, boys . . . "

But he made the next one last. He had no intention of getting into a tourist-like condition himself. For what lay ahead he wanted to be tanked up just right and no more.

"Thanks again, boys, here's to you . . . now where was I? Oh yeh, was just going to tell you-all about the great importance of wrist work in my trade. I'll tell you a li'll secret about that. You may have spotted how I allus keep my arms folded while the deppities are chousin' 'em up the steps to me. That's a thing I do a-purpose, folding my arms at that percise point. It lets me flex my wrists without the crowd noticin', see? And I'll let you boys in on another secret of the hangin' trade. When I — "

Suddenly a flurry of revolver shots popped faintly outside the bar's steamed-over plate glass front. And then came a few more. The hangman cut off his contemptuous tourist talk in mid-flow, leaping to his feet. He rushed away from the ring of amazed slack faces out to the riverfront, pulling his large old double pistols as he went.

Two more shots sounded. (Heavier

ones? No, that couldn't be — they just sounded heavier now he was outside.) Those last, interspersed with some lusty screams, had come like all the rest from the direction of First Street.

He cornered up there like a champion pacer, dodging between a couple of parked carriages on the near curb to cross over to the parlor houses side. There, he sprinted along the walk and threw himself up the steps to The Riverboat House.

9

THE proprietress herself came reeling down the staircase at that moment, hanging on to the rail with her long claws.

"*Lansakes, Maledon, thank God you got here!*" she uttered in a quavering voice he had to admire. "*There's a gunfight on the upper floor!*"

"Slack off, sweetheart, there ain't no call to play the minstrel at me," he whispered irritably as he shoved past her on his way up. Then the breath whooshed out of him as he took in that word *gunfight*, meaning guns plural. He recalled the varying sounds of the explosions outside. And he also now took in that Miss Rosa Lou had turned ashen in a convincing style that no minstrel on Earth could have managed to pretend.

He glared at her on the darkening

lampless stairs. "Look, woman, if you've doubled me in some cute way I swear I'll — !"

"It's nothin' like that, you fool!" she hissed back hysterically. "I did it just as we planned! *Only that half-ass clerk packed a stingy gun, didn't he!*"

"Oh Jesus," he muttered unsteadily. He half-turned and began jumping up the stairs three at a time to the first hallway, with the madam moaning and wailing at his heels.

The gunfire from the top storey had ceased now; but he knew before he got up there that those two last different shots had come from a double-derringer. As he gained the top floor he saw a door slanting into the passage, hanging by one hinge. Holding his breath he jumped spraddle-legged into the aperture beside it, holding out his two ancient sidearms like a somewhat oldtime gunsharp.

The sight that met his bugging gaze was not what he'd planned; not what he'd planned at all . . .

At the close of his previous visit here Rosa Lou had told him about the clerk's taste for young she-stuff. He had fallen in readily with her suggestion that they made use of that to rig the trap for him. It was arranged that she would hire a town loafer of her acquaintance, and have him bust in on the clerk with a weapon, raving as he did so that he was the girl's outraged father. He was supposed to fire a few outraged shots at the ceiling, which would bring George Maledon (happening nearby) on the run. And then he would manage to 'pacify' the distraught parent by an impressive show of authority, and spirit the unnerved clerk away from The Riverboat House by way of the outside stairs; later concluding an arrangement with him based on what had taken place.

It looked as though the loafer had tried to play his part in the scheme with too much enthusiasm. About half the ceiling had come down, mostly on to the cavernous whorehouse bed where

Higgs and his young companion were still seated rigidly side by side like a couple of snow models. The only un-white objects in that part of the smallish room were the clerk's wildly distended dark eyes, and the darker twin holes of the little weapon that was still gripped, as though by rigor mortis, in his hand.

The hangman's stricken glance wavered off the two of them down to the floor itself. The first of those stingy blasts had gone by the loafer and punched out the door. The second one had kicked a hole in his chest like a dynamite crater. He lay there on his back stone dead, amongst the contrasting colors of the white and red-spreading plaster he had fallen on.

His senses whirled. He screeched at the paralyzed clerk: "*You crazy murdersome sonofabitch!*" Then he grabbed hold of the weeping proprietress. "*I still make it you somehow did this, you — you — !*"

She angrily shook herself loose. She

was still very pale, but calmer now.

"Of course I didn't," she murmured quietly. "And keep your voice down. Do you want to blow the whole thing with the clerk there?"

"It got blown the moment he dug for that purse gun," he ground out bitterly.

The face of the proprietress grew tigerish. "Oh no it didn't. I don't intend to have a scandal here if you do, hangerman."

Approaching steps could now be heard on the staircase, and the alarmed voices of both sexes. Rosa Lou took a deep breath and moved quickly out to the hallway. "It's all right, folks," she called down in a steady voice. "Just a drunk cleanin' his gun. No harm's done." The not overly curious steps and voices retreated.

Then she came back in the room, dragging the mangled door almost closed behind her. By then the Prince of Hangmen too was starting to calm down. He said quietly: "Can you get to your outside steps by that window? I seem to recall your top flight goes up on that side."

She gave a mute nod, shoving a bunch of hair off her face which had loosened from its celluloid grips in the excitement. About half of her high birdsnest was still in place. The sight of the man she had hired to his death was turning her green about the gills once more. She exclaimed suddenly and intensely to herself: "*Why couldn't this of happened to Mrs Aaron P. Wodis . . .*"

Maledon touched her heaving shoulder. "Don't fret over him on the floor. I'll take care of him. I'll pack him out once it's dark by the open steps. But right now what needs doin' is we shift the clerk."

He moved to the bedside and prised Higgs's stiff fingers from the deadly little weapon, putting it in his pocket. Then he knocked enough chunks of plaster off the quilt to be able to peel back the covers. And then he just stared and swore for a space.

The fixed-gazing young girl was wearing the style of colorful falderals that he personally shined to — on grown women. On her, though, the effect was quite different. She reminded him of Annie a bit, when his daughter had been around that same age. He grated out: "You alive in there, honey?"

"Yes, sir," she whispered back. But she didn't sound too certain. She sounded as though Crawford Higgs, and a shooting scrape, and a bombardment of plaster, and finally a corpse bleeding all over the floor, had proved too strenuous for this early stage of her apprenticeship.

He jerked his head angrily behind him at the madam. "For God's sake get this merchandise out of here, woman. Damn it all, when you said *young* I never suspicioned you meant *this* young . . . "

"Maledon, Maledon," Rosa said in a weary tone as if she were addressing someone of the age of the child in the bed. "I know that a body on my floor means about the same to you as a heap of horseshit. But in the eyes of the world he's what matters! *Nothin' else here matters but him and I want him gone!*"

He looked away from her back at the bed; but not before, to her amazement, she had caught a wet shine on those death-dealing eyes.

"That's your opinion, sweetheart," he said huskily. "We won't argue it right now. Come and try to make her snap to again, if that's possible. And if the house can stand it I should see she gets some rest, was I you."

Rosa Lou tossed him an odd glance. That the court hangman might have some stray feelings was a possibility which had never struck her before. She had been about to say something typically brass-tipped back to him, but now she gave the distinctive shrug of her kind and came over and began to hen her chick.

Gradually the girl began to shiver and shake in her arms, and then to keen like a squaw. Rosa groped around on the floor for her dress, finally pulling it free of wreckage in a cloud of white dust. George Maledon began to feel better once that skinny and half-formed body was decently covered and out of sight.

As the two of them made for the door and squeezed past it he called quietly after them: "Make damn sure no one comes up here in the next hour."

And then, once left alone with him, he concentrated all his attention on the naked figure of Crawford Higgs. He wouldn't have believed that he could think any worse of him than before, but the last few minutes had seen to that. He slapped him twice, with satisfaction, across his rigidly held face.

"Well now, Mister Clerk," he said with mocking formality as those oily brown pebbles began to slide around again. "Appears like you're in a peck of trouble, wouldn't you say?" He dabbed his chin sombrely at the corpse.

"I — I thought he was firing at me," Higgs muttered as though from some distant and far-off place. "He kept yelling out he was her father and — and I've had some difficulties with kinfolk before. That's why I always take my gun to these — these places . . . Where is my gun?"

"I just took it from you. I've got to get you shed of here, Mr Clerk, or else you'll bring down some, uh, illfame on the court, I'm thinking. So let's get you back in your close first, uh? Where are your goddam close? — oh, seems they're under some more of the ceiling here." He began shaking another fog of dust out of the clerk's suit pants.

"*Was* that crazy fellow really her father?" Higgs whimpered when he had him about half-dressed.

George Maledon worked up his first faint grin for some while. He was beginning to see that this drastic turnout to his plan had one good side to it at least: he didn't have the clerk caught in just a double-cinch as he'd schemed to. He had him shut in a total box, once he'd got him safely away from here.

He wagged his grizzled head at him sadly. "That don't hardly signify now, Higgs. He may or may not of been a father before, but he sure as hell ain't gonna be one in future. It's a powerful luckstreak for you I chanced by, and none of them state police harness bulls as are supposed to patrol on The Row. Had they showed up, your goose would have been cooked. But out a my loyalty to the court I'll fix to come back later and clean up this whole mess for you. Right now, though, finish gettin' dressed and let's put this sorry affair in back of us."

★ ★ ★

The court clerk had looked a bit like a dudish bakery hand, even after they'd both done what they could to knock the plaster dust out of his hat and suiting.

Maledon un-catched the window and shoved it up on its cords, thinking to take him out by way of the open stairs, as a sort of live rehearsal for the dead run later. Not that Crawford Higgs had come all that much alive yet. When he bade him take a turn or two of the room, he seemed pretty wobbly for going out the window. He guessed it wasn't so much a case of his legs being shaken as his mind.

"We'd bestways go down through the house," he decided with snarling reluctance. "Though what I'm thinkin' is there's a certain risk if we're noticed by someone, what with *your victim* bein' still up here."

The clerk seemed to turn a paler shade yet under his coat of dust. Maledon tugged the window down until it was almost closed but for leaving him a grip on it from the outside. Then he helped Higgs past the door wreckage to the dark landing.

They passed a sputtering lamp on each of the other floors, but The Riverboat House seemed to be going through an unwontedly quiet space for the time of night. The hangman guessed that Rosa Lou might have closed shop generally, rather than just barring off the top storey as he'd told her. It took plenty of ruckus to make a Row madam close shop in a hurry — but a messy murder might have done it.

That surmise proved to be true; when they came to the entrance door, still without passing a soul on the way, both its heavy locks had been turned and the flat metal bar had been slotted across its width.

He grimaced to himself as he took the bar off and unturned the locks. It hadn't struck him until now, but it was a fact that if a man had to be stuck with an illegal unhanged body, on his hands, a well-fortified parlor house wasn't the worst place for it by any means. He hoped Rosa Lou was listening close by, and would re-lock and bar after they had left.

He walked the clerk halfway up First Street, until he was sure he'd get home all right under his own power. Then he said pleasantly: "I'll say good night now, Mister Clerk." And then — a shade less pleasantly — "I'll be sure to stop by your office in the morning and report how I handled the corpse, sir."

Crawford Higgs peered at him in the darkness, looking now more like a dudish whitened ghost than a bakery hand. "There's no need I assure you," he gabbled miserably. "I have every confidence in you, Maledon. I'm obliged — most obliged — for everything you've undertaken for me."

"I'll stop by," he repeated in a certain tone.

The clerk nodded more miserably still. "Yes — yes, of course you will. I shall be expecting you. Goodnight now."

George Maledon watched him scuttle off into the night with a sense of deep satisfaction. For there — unless he missed his guess — went one highly alarmed and helpless eastern spy.

It was just a matter now of using him to the greatest possible benefit all round . . .

★ ★ ★

He turned back toward the river, to deal with the dead man, with a feeling of considerably reduced tension; though vaguely aware that most folks wouldn't see it that way.

But what with the night being so black, and the river so handy and close to spate with all this rain they'd had, he didn't reckon on meeting any trouble with the loafer without he did something damned stupid, or was just sheerly out of luck.

In point of fact it went off just as easy as he'd thought, or better. When he climbed the outer stairs of The Riverboat House, and let himself into the death room by the top window, in the meantime Rosa Lou had got the loafer's corpse dragged on to a black tarp. She'd left a length of string by it and washed up the floor around him. He only had to tie him in the tarp and bundle him through the window, then hop out after him.

"One-sixty odd," he mumbled automatically as he shouldered his burden and started with care down the steep-treaded wooden steps.

George Maledon himself weighed distinctly less than that, but he was used to such carrying. Leaving the steps, he glided smoothly across the weed and trash-strewn yard behind the house until he came to its bottom fence, which also bordered a narrow zig-zagging cut to the river front.

The cut was in total darkness, but he hesitated to shove the corpse over the fence. He knew the cut was popular with Row women trying to skim off some extra under the madam's nose. He didn't aim to test out the three's-a-crowd theory with the loafer just now.

He put him down instead and began hunting along the fence for some loose boards. Some were sheer pulpwood, where the bottom fence joined with the divider between The Riverboat House lot and the piece behind Madame June's Salon. He worked them out quietly with his strong arms, taking care not to splinter any and make a noise. When three were removed the gap was just big enough for him and his companion to pass through.

He found there was no un-house business being transacted there that night. He just bore the loafer on down to the Arkansas, swiftly crossing the embankment road between two of its evenly spaced rings of lampshine.

There was a nearby go-down to the river used for watering horses and launching catfish boats. He used it now to launch the loafer; pausing there until he and his tarp shroud showed no longer in the blurred patches that glittered the swirling inshore water.

★ ★ ★

Next day, he made a point of combing his wild beard, and shining his boots to glassy perfection, before he knocked on the clerk's door in the middle forenoon. He aimed to do this in some style.

Crawford Higgs was in the middle of dictating some notes to a stenographer at that moment; and, as he sweated so much in normal circumstances, there was no knowing if the sight of himself was bringing on a bigger rush of it. But he fancied it was. He grunted amiably: "I'll look in later, Mister Clerk."

"No — no, come in, Maledon. Meg — that will be all for now . . . "

"Be seated," he said with a stretched grin when they were alone.

"No need, sir, this won't take but a moment to say out."

"As you wish. But before you commence, Maledon, I wish to make clear I have considered my obligation to you at some length overnight and — "

163

"I bet," he cut in with sudden harshness. He tongued his pipe aside and hawked on the clerk's floor.

"Er, yes, and I feel that some expression — some tangible expression — of my indebtedness to you is certainly due."

He bared his teeth around the stem. "You do, uh? Glad to see you didn't lose them nose lenses of yours in all that mess of plaster. Though mebbe you don't take your lenses when you go off relaxing." He spat again. "Figures when you think it through."

Crawford Higgs eyed him with matching hostility. "You don't much like me, do you," he said quietly.

"No shit, Mister Clerk."

"Well I feel much the same about you. But it doesn't signify in this situation — unless it makes you unreasonable, that is. I'm willing to be bled by you over what happened *just once and in reason*. Don't overlook that you're tied in this with me to some degree. Er, I take it you did dispose of our friend successfully?"

"Sure. Go on with what you're sayin'."

"What I'm saying, Maledon, is if you kick me down, I'll make damned sure I hang on to your boot." A venomous gleam was now coming through those glasses at him.

"Let's don't get ahead of ourselfs," he murmured softly. "Was you really notional I'd want a pay-off just for doin' my duty by the court? Not me, sir. No, all I had in mind was just a small good turn from you. But a course, iffen that's not proper for me to ask we'll forget that also."

He grinned in a way that the puzzled clerk did not find reassuring.

"What kind of a good turn?" he asked suspiciously. "I'd *prefer* to give you money to anything else — though as I say, in reason."

"Yeh, the way I read you you would prefer that. Only that ain't what I want from you. What I want is a helpin' hand to get His Honor out of town on a certain day. Is that too much to ask, sir? You just speak out if it is."

The court clerk was silent for a long moment; while his enlarged brown marbles asked all sorts of questions, and considered all sorts of answers to each. Then he shook his head firmly.

"No, it's more than my job is worth to — to go behind the judge's back in any way whatever. I haven't been here long, but I've learned that well enough."

George Maledon moved slightly toward the door. "That's all right, Mister Clerk. My, what a nice day it's turnin' out. Think I'll take a walk later on in some fresh part of town I ain't seen lately. Must be nice over where you are on Fourth. Eunice — that's my wife, sir — was saying to me only yesterday what a right smart little home you got yourself there."

His tone took on a more rasping edge. "An' a right smart little wife to go with it too, by all account. A course, these court women, they get lonesome left on their own so much, don' they? Don' I hear that enough from Eunice! Heh-heh! Though my own view is that makes 'em sociable inclined more'n most womenfolk, iffen they get half a chance."

He broke off to puff balefully at the clerk's darkening visage. "Me, I'm allus sociable. Like nothin' better than to find I'm in a dooryard conversation on a nice afternoon when I never expected one."

He broke off again and stared idly out the window at the courthouse square.

"What exactly did you want done concerning the judge?" Higgs asked presently, as though each of those words coming out of him was on the end of a surgeon's tongs.

"Oh, you're back to that again, sir, are you? Well, the thing is he's got a son called Charlie doin' law school in Saint Lou. Kind of a temper'mental boy, Charlie allus was. Up one minute an' down the next, y'know the kind?

Now, the thing is if His Honor was to get a telegram full of suicide talk from Charlie, sent all convincing from Saint Lou, there's no question it would fetch him up there on the run."

"I don't know a single soul in that town," Higgs grunted pettishly.

The hangman shrugged. "There's trains. The Smith an' Little Rock takes you up there in a jiff."

"Then why don't you go up and send it to him yourself?"

"Because I don't choose to, that's why. I'll have a lot to see to down here at that time." He paused, and nailed the clerk with a feisty glare. "And also I guess because I never got myself in dutch by killin' anyone with a purse gun."

"Is that *it*?" Higgs asked slowly. "Is that all I have to do to hold you off from telling my wife about — about yesterday?"

"Not quite. You've also got to fix Parker's schedule so he ain't got a murder case to try around the time of the date I'll give you. Since if he did have his teeth into a murder case at that time, he just might let Charlie take his chances."

"You seem to know a whole lot about his affairs as well as mine," Crawford Higgs observed with some bitterness. "How can I be sure you'll get off my back if I do this for you?"

He shrugged again. "Like you say, I'm in the same vice you are, up to a point. I don't plan to finish up on the wrong side of my own gibbet. You do this and the two of us are square, far as I'm concerned," he finished deliberately.

"Have you got this boy's Saint Louis address with you now?"

"Why, I do believe I have, sir. Here it is."

"And what's the date when you want the judge to be away from here?"

"Twelfth of next month. The afternoon of Tuesday the twelfth. Which means he'd ought to get the wire not sooner nor later than first thing that morning, to fit my purpose. You'll need to layover in Saint Lou, Mister Clerk."

"All right, I'll do it. Though why you should want this out of me instead of dollars I can't imagine. I think nearly all you people down here are bigoted half crazy relics from the past, if you want my opinion."

"Can't say as I do," he murmured as he made for the door. He hung back there. "Oh, by the way, the boy don't call his pa *dad*. That whole fambly act kind of stiff together. Make the 'gram start off *My dear father*. And wind up with *Your affectionate son*. The kid writes home in that style. You word the in between how you choose. You're a lettered fellow, and should be a fair hand at quality language. But I suggest you have Charlie say he's scared he'll never make into a top lawyer like Isaac — which is only the plain truth, come to that."

He gave the clerk a cold dismissive nod and left him.

10

HE had felt a bit queasy after that session with Crawford Higgs.

Not because he feared that the killer and child-fancier was in any position to double him; it was what Parker might do if the scheme turned sour that had sent the chill crawling through his guts.

It had seemed a pretty clever notion when it first struck him; taking care of his own problem along with Isaac's, by having that faked suicide wire arrive on the date he had chosen for the record attempt. But if it was ever found out who was behind sending the telegram, he was bleakly sure that his days as a government executioner would be over.

That was why he'd forced the clerk to go up to Missouri to handle the actual sending. He aimed to make himself highly noticeable to Parker in the time before he got the wire, so he would be less likely to connect him with it afterward.

But the queasy feeling went farther than that. It was being borne in on him that Zeb Allen's cheap stunt of a speed hanging had now gotten himself into serious deep shit. And he had a nasty feeling that substance was apt to grow deeper yet, until his record try was over and — hopefully — done with.

That foreboding was much increased a few days later, at the drag end of September.

He'd done three more jobs in the square by then; just solos. And although he'd taken pains not to allow the slightest taint of levity to mar those despatchings, he had found himself setting his watch on them, and hustling up his re-slanted ladder faster than he'd been wont to do before he'd heard of Allen's fool stunt. But he saw no harm in getting in a bit of warm-up practice for the attempt — so long as it didn't show either to Parker, watching as always from his window, or to the yokels in the scanty crowds which those dull solo drops pulled in.

As far as the judge was concerned, he was fairly sure his slight changes from normal procedure passed unnoticed; and most of the tourists would have been too ignorant to notice there was anything out of the way going on either. But as it turned out, there were one or two watchers down there who weren't that ignorant — or that unobservant.

On the last Friday of every month (unless it crossed with Christmas), George Maledon went to his local branch meet of the Grand Army of the Republic.

The Grand Army was a Union veterans' association; and although Arkansas had been on the other side at the time, enough of General Grant's old campaigners were living in that area to ensure a steady, if small, attendance for the meets. In early years after the conflict they had been enlivened by short further outbreaks between the lodge members and their aggravated Fort Smith neighbors. But all that leftover antagonism had itself passed into ancient history by 1890. The lodge now existed simply for a bunch of oldtimers to get together and re-hash their common past.

The hangman usually enjoyed the meets. He was something of a local celebrity at them. Most of his pals there had run down dismally over the years, to become storekeepers and bank tellers and suchlike no-accounts. He was one of the few of them whose lives had looked up when the war was over.

That fact was acknowledged in various ways: he had his own, better chair beside the stove; his own sabre-engraved pewter tankard on its separate high shelf above the back bar (when it wasn't being kept clean and filled up by a watchful steward); — and, most gratifying of all, his own opinions were sought regularly on any subject that remotely involved death.

When he came in on the evening of the last Friday in September, two of his pals were already at their usual table. Spud Appleby and Dieter Heinz.

That pair weren't usually the hail-fellow kind. But tonight they called out to him at once.

"Hey, Prince, come on over! What you kickin' off with? — I'll get it!"

"Just the usual, thanks, Dee," he mumbled in faint surprise. He took his usual chair and rocked some. Funny: doing that habitual thing didn't seem to make him feel homey right away, the way it usually did. He glanced over at the two old Springfields that were criss-crossed over the bar, and at Pete Simmons polishing his glassware underneath them. Everything seemed the same.

"You feelin' chipper tonight, George?" Spud was saying brightly, in a sort of prying way that sounded a bit strong for the sentiment expressed.

"I'm okay," he grunted. "Overworked as usual. That ol' bastard don't give me much rest these days what with all he sends out to me."

It was only at the lodge meets that he would speak thus of Parker. Sometimes he felt he needed these evenings in order to mildly badmouth the Old Man at them; it was the other side of his coin of devotion to him.

"You look pretty much okay," Spud agreed consideringly. "Don't he look okay, Dee? I was just sayin' . . . " he broke off as Dieter Heinz got in the three beers.

Heinz set them down and regarded George Maledon with the same slight air of over-intensity he'd noticed in Spud's attitude. "I dunno," he pronounced finally, as he slacked into one of the standard issue non-rockers which bore the Grand Army shield on their uncomfortable backs. "He might look a bit peeked round the eyes since last month."

"I ain't peeked at all," the hangman

said crossly. "Only overworked, like I was jus' saying."

"The way I heard it, you've only been doing 'em on their own lately," said Dieter Heinz. He shook his cropped greying head a little. "If you're gettin' peeked on only that — " He took a pensive swig from his glass.

"You feel like shootin' some pool in a minute, George?" Spud said next. "I'll go clear some a the boys off a table if you do. All them tables in the other room are taken early this time. But they'll be proud to clear one for you, that's for sure."

Maledon shot Spud Appleby a narrow-eyed glance over the top of his private tankard. He was used to a certain amount of deference from his old army buddies. He knew it tickled them plenty to be able to swap old battle yarns with the Prince of Hangmen in person. But he didn't cut such a big swath with them that pool fanatics would willingly butt out from a match, just because he felt like trying his indifferent skills. He was becoming definitely curious now about the expression in both Spud's and Dieter's lined faces.

"I don't often pick up a cue in back," he growled thoughtfully. "Why should tonight be any different?"

Spud seemed at a slight loss. "Well . . . I guess I dunno. I guess I just figgered you might like to stay sharp, y'know? I mean, you don't want to just set there all night drinkin', do you?"

"Why don' I?" he asked bluntly. "It's what we all come here for, iffen we tell the truth. That and to get shed of the women for a space, and recollec' them good ol' days afore they got their hooks in us."

That thought made him try to turn the talk in a more conventional direction. "Say, Dee, was you at Aunty-tam Crick that time? I know Spud was, but now I try to place you at that scrap I ain't sure whether you was there or not."

Heinz frowned. "No, I wasn't. I got drafted too late for that. And any road,

George, you shouldn't be dwellin' on the war tonight, should he, Spud? If a man dwells overmuch on that war, even this long after, he can still get morbid. And George can't afford to get morbid on top of bein' peeked already. Well, any road, *I* can't afford him to," Heinz finished up with another grave headshake.

The hangman set down his tankard with a thump. "What's goin' on atween you pair of bozos? What's all this continued bulljuice about my health? And whatinhell d'you mean, Dieter, about not bein' able to afford it iffen I was ailing — *which I repeat I ain't!*"

"Stay calm, George," Spud said urgently. He cast a look of wonderment at Heinz. "He don't know," he said softly. "I do believe he don't know . . . "

"He knows, he's just ridin' us," Heinz scoffed. He looked in a dubious way at the hangman's tankard. "I'd get you another, Prince, only I ain't sure as you should."

"*What is this?*" Maledon roared, so

that Pete Simmons dropped a half-polished glass with a broken clatter behind his shelf. "You dumbos had better let me in on this josh afore I like to break your necks!"

"I guess we had ought to tell him," Spud said somewhat hastily. For there was something about their small companion that stopped him from ever sounding quite humorous, on the rare occasions when he spoke lightly of breaking necks.

"Yeh," Heinz agreed. "I guess we'd ought. Come to that it ain't right he shouldn't know, if he really don't — not with the whole damn lodge plunged on him like it is now."

In the short, tingling silence that followed, George Maledon began to see the outline of the shocking truth. "Are you saying," he muttered thickly, "are you fools saying there's an actual book got up on my — my hangin' contest with that sonofabitch Zebediah Allen?"

"You better believe that," Heinz

assured him gravely. He shrugged. "Not that I got any complaints myself so far. I could have got you at seven an' four. But somethin' told me you'd fade off, and so you did, after that last poor ladder run. Tim Holt was there representin' the lodge when you did that last ladder run. He timed you a good two secs slower'n the time you skipped up there before. That's how come I got you at six an' four."

The hangman's shaken features were now slowly altering and becoming suffused with color. "*Seven and four?*" he bellowed furiously. "*Six and four?* Well, ain't that wonderful, I must say! *Some pals* I got in this lodge! Jesus H. Christ! Six and four! — *and against a jack leg lyncher like that Zeb!*"

His feelings then overwhelmed and choked him, and he slammed back and forth in his rocker, just turkey-gobbling to himself incoherently.

Spud and Dieter exchanged alarmed glances. "Now whatever you do don't go over-straining yourself," Spud cautioned; but that piece of self-serving goodwill only drew him a look of pure molten lava which made that tough old soldier turn quite pallid.

His rage over the insulting odds didn't last long. It was driven out by a sense of real alarm. He tried to frame his next remarks in a way that might draw an answer to soothe that alarm.

He gave a short husky laugh. "Yeh, well, I guess that was bound to happen. Of course, it ain't a proper matter to bet on an event like a hangin'. But I guess so long as it's kept to the lodge, and to boys like you who can spare a few pennies, I guess that's not apt to be overly harmful . . . " He paused hopefully, showing a tentative grin.

But the faces of Spud Appleby and Dieter Heinz did not grin back. "*Pennies?*" Dee echoed him loudly. "*Kept to the lodge?*" Spud said in much the same marvelling tone. "George — you just don't know . . . "

"What don't I know?" he murmured

grimly. "And quit guying me over it. I want to know all that's been done behind my back concernin' this antic."

"Well," Spud told him with a heavy sigh, "here she is, then. There's three definite books on you, to my knowing. There's ours in the lodge, there's one in the Chamber of Commerce, and there's another been got up by the boys in the First National. But that's only the top a the heap, I'm sure. If I had to, huh, bet on it, I'd say there's books on you got up all over the city now. And there's no question of penny limits — not with ours here, anyhow. Seriously, George, there's the kind of stakes ridin' on you in this lodge what can't be afforded to lose in most cases. Dee here went five hundred on you. I went . . . well, somewhat above that. I don't know a single soul who went on you below a couple hundred. There's some high ones who used collateral too. It's that kind of a deal, George. Now maybe you see why we're sort of anxious you should be in shape for the day. When *is* the goddam day to be? I hope to God it's soon, because I'm sweatin' that much weight off me I won't *be here* if it don't happen soon . . . "

At that particular dire moment, who should come slowly down the single step from the other room than the lodge's oldest member, one 'Uncle Greg' Cisneros, who had gone with Sherman on his blood-soaked sweep to the sea. He always wore a tattered blue uniform and fatigue cap to the meets, and he tended to live back in that world most of his time. But not right now, it seemed.

"George, boy!" the oldtimer called out as he hobbled forward to the three of them at the table. "I claim it proud that I just got on you at fives, George!" he cackled gleefully. "Staked all my allotment for the next twelve-month! You don't aim to let me down, son, do you?" He swayed skinnily above them, his glee suddenly crumpling so that he looked drawn and worried and older than ever.

The Prince of Hangmen had now gone very white. He stood up, looking bitterly in turn at Appleby and Heinz and the oldtimer. "*You pluperfect fools,*" he said under his breath. Then he wheeled and marched out of the lodge hall, with a faltering and unsoldierly stride.

* * *

At first, he still had such a mad on that he told himself it was all their own damned fault. If the odds had been set sensibly, they wouldn't have drawn such reckless — and maybe ruinous — folly. The notion that there were any so-called sane men in this town who actual thought of setting *fifty-fifty* between him and Zeb, was enough to make him pop every vein in his body . . .

But as had happened before in the hall, he sobered down again when he got thinking of what all these bets would mean to him personally.

185

Word of them would get back to Parker. If there was a book going in a hightone circle like the Chamber of Commerce, then it was only a matter of time before one of the Old Man's dinner chums brought it righteously to his attention . . .

He felt sick with fear as he stomped home through the dark streets, toward the new fizzing white lights above Garrison Avenue. It had been bad enough to consider what Parker might do about it if he only learned there was a speed record involved. *But how about a speed record that was also being gambled on all over the city?*

He knew exactly how the judge looked on gambling. It was included on his personal shit list of major crimes, along with killing and compulsory poontang.

. . . He would just have to call the whole thing off somehow. After all, if he *called* it off, then all those dumb-minded and unfitting bets would goddam *be* off, wouldn't they . . . ?

But how could that be done this late? He'd already whipsawed that bastard of a court clerk to go up to Saint Lou and send Isaac that crazy wire. (Which was enough to earn him a pull in some federal prison just by itself, leaving out all this other new mess . . .)

He groaned aloud as he turned off Garrison on to the renewed blackness of North Thirteenth. That groan did not stem entirely from his turmoil of desperate thoughts. For his home street wasn't in total darkness. Halfway down it, past his own house, a lamp was burning up on the Old Man's second floor.

He wondered despondently what he was doing. Maybe just reading in bed or something. Or — just as likely — getting a gambling case put finally together for tomorrow's court sessions . . .

With another deep heartfelt groan, he unlatched his yard gate and hastened up the path away from that boding and accusing yellow gleam.

11

BUT a surprisingly good night's sleep made his brain work more clearly and calmly in the morning.

What he'd overlooked in his first shock was the fact that Parker was in many ways an almost incredibly unworldly man. If one of his dinner companions should chance to say that his court executioner had a book going on him, he doubted that phrase would mean much to him. And even if it was put plainer than that, well, the Old Man relied on him a smart amount just now, to help get shed of Crawford Higgs. He wouldn't be wishful of flaying the hide off him before that other piece of business was seen to first. And after it he could hardly avoid being grateful to him, howsoever angry he was over the bets.

No: just as long as he could keep him from seeing the record attempt, and then tossed the clerk to him right after it for insurance, like he planned to, he didn't reckon he stood in much danger from the Old Man now that he had thought it through.

And in the light of day even those heavy lodge bets didn't seem such a worrisome burden to him either. For no matter what damnfool odds his faithless old pals were setting on him, he hadn't a shadow of doubt that he would lick Zeb off the board when the time came to do that.

. . . Not that those idiots who set the lodge book didn't maybe have *half* of a point when they'd eased off him after that last practice sprint up the ladder, he allowed grudgingly. It was true his legs still weren't fast enough. That wasn't his fault. He had put in a sight of effort with a skip-rope, every evening in his workshop for the past week or more. But he never had been much at running and jumping — arm power was his strong suit. He just couldn't figure a better way to get more snap into his legs if the skip-rope wouldn't do that.

George Maledon didn't know it, but a drastically better method was soon to be revealed to him.

★ ★ ★

However, before that revelation occurred, two days later at suppertime he gradually grew aware that the whole speed-hanging project was threatening to get out of control.

That 'gradually' had to do with his wife and daughter. He hadn't hanged anyone that day, but as he chomped his way morosely through a (damned cheap cut) steak and some (half-boiled) collard greens, the punishing nature of that grub, plus the oppressive silence at the table, made him gradually sense that he was somehow in dutch again with his womenfolk.

That suspicion proved up once Annie

had taken herself pointedly upstairs. Eunice then started in on him at once.

"What's all this foolishness I hear about folks bettin' on you? Don't you feel you bring enough shame down on this family as it is, George? What are these bets about? — and don't try not telling me, because I intend to get to the bottom of this in the end . . . "

His thick fingers tightened on the knife and fork. "So *that's* how come I got this muck to eat," he said drily. "I might of known."

Eunice Maledon pushed back a loose strand of her bunned grey-black hair, and placed her wash-reddened hands akimbo on her wide apron'd hips.

"It's a sight better than you deserve," she continued in the same fractious tone. "*Bets*, indeed! And I haven't a doubt in my head in your case that means bets on *it*, doesn't it? You may as well admit that's what it means!" At that point she threw in a gulpy sob which, he knew from past experience, was the advance scout of many more to follow.

"George, I really am surprised even at you! Haven't you considered what will happen if the judge finds out? Oh, I guess you think you're that close to him it won't matter — but it *will*, you know! I don't like that man and never have, but I will own he's a good Christian where the evil of gambling is concerned. Why, when I only think on what happened to my poor brother . . . *and* his family! How could you be so stupid, George? *Oh — it's the last straw really it is!*"

And with that she clapped her hands to her plump downy face, and got started on the kind of steady snivelling bawl that she'd perfected over the years as the two of them had aged together.

"A course I know all that, woman," he ground out. "Are you dumb enough to figure it was *me* as wanted the sorry levity of books bein' set on a serious matter like a hangin'? A course I never did! Iffen you want to find someone to blame for it, go buy yourself a ticket to Philly and blame Zeb Allen! About the las' thing I ever wanted was for gambles goin' down on my job! It was them lunkheads from the Grand Lodge as got this contest atween me'n Zeb cheapened the way it's gone now! But it ain't *my* goddam fault!"

He broke off to wag a finger at her stormy countenance. "The trouble with you, Euny, is you jump in half-cock to take other folks' part against me, without ever pausing to ponder there just might be somethin' to say on *my end . . .* "

"*Somethin' to say on your end,*" she mocked him harshly. "How could there be? You're a hangman — a lifetaker! And now you're — you're touched with the mortal sin of gambling too!"

"Let's don't fetch up that idiot uncle a yourn," he grunted sourly, shoving the unfinished plateful violently across the board. "There's all the difference in the world from a fellow havin' bets put on him against his wish, and that half-ass old fool settin' out to ruin his fambly on some sharper's blanket at a country fair."

"*Don't you dare say one word against my uncle! Just don't you dare!* I'm — I'm going upstairs now because I'm too upset to speak any more about it, George . . . *No — you keep your blood-stained hands off me!*"

With a final loud snivel, Eunice skittered around his restraining arms, and began to pound up the squealing boards of the stairs that she liked to remind him still weren't fixed.

He slammed himself down in his easychair, groping grimly for his pipe. . . . He should have known those damned bets would get tattled over the fences. *Well, let them be*, he told himself with a sudden rush of pugnacity. *He* didn't care worth a durn what a pack of ignorant women thought, or didn't think, about this professional contest between him and Allen. So long as he could get it past the judge without being fired

194

off the job, other people could make of it what they pleased — whether they were stupid old soldiers or stupid women . . .

He lit up, drawing in fiercely. At that moment his daughter came down again to the livingroom. She said in her grown-up snippish tones: "You've gone and overset ma now."

He snatched out his pipe and leveled it at her with a pent-up quiver.

"Now just you hobble your lip, girly . . . I ain't in a mood for it just now, I tell you . . . "

Annie Maledon cocked her thin freckled face on one side. She put her hands on her narrow hips as her mother had just been doing more amply. "Oh, I wouldn't dream of speaking out of turn, father," she said in a peculiar creamy tone. "I wouldn't dream of getting into a private scrap between parents, the very idea!"

He glowered up at her suspiciously. "You wouldn't, uh? It'd be about the first time ever, then."

Annie ignored that and sat down at the table. She smoothed her shirt-waist and gave him a faint smile; for the first time in many a long day.

"You shouldn't pay too much mind to mother, y'know," she said softly, in her old confiding way that could still turn a sudden spearhead of buried memory deep inside him. "I reckon she's still sore on that subject after what Uncle Rolf went an' did."

"But you see it different, is that what you're sayin'?" he mumbled in gruff astonishment.

Annie Maledon sat in undecided silence for a moment. They both knew that she nearly always took her mother's side in the frequent family spats. She felt it was ladylike to share her mother's anti-hanging opinions; and to a certain extent she shared them honestly, because life had not been easy on her as the Prince of Hangmen's daughter.

Once she'd got her growth, that awkward position had irked her a considerable piece. She felt it was a bad enough outlook for her being plainish and unrich, without having the men she could attract take off in a rush once her pa had touched them and looked into their eyes.

Probably George Maledon didn't consciously intend that dire effect upon most of his daughters young men. But he had been very close to her when she was a child, and a certain critical tendency had perhaps been apparent when he shook their hands, and tried to crack a smile at the latest supplanter of his own onetime position in Annie's regard.

Whether that was so or not, the cruel fact was that they had all tended to reconsider the relationship once that stumbling point in it was reached. (All except the married one in Little Rock, whom her father had discouraged more positively in the end.)

Right now she had a boy on her string who seemed very promising: a city alderman's son. But, of course, she knew that his station in life wasn't promising in the least for a mere working stiff's daughter. The solitary gleam of hope in it for her lay in the fact that Arnold Harper's folks were poor by alderman's standards. He had let that slip to her quite a few times — along with one or two other slips besides.

So what with one thing and another, while echoing her mother's outrage as usual, she had learned of this betting affair with a certain degree of thoughtful reflection. Being a provident girl, by now she had a small nest egg saved from her various short-time jobs about the city, and set by against the time when she would leave home. It had struck her forcibly that if her nest egg could be made more substantial in a hurry, it just might be enough to grease her way toward becoming Mrs Arnold Harper. That possible solution to her problem lay behind the serious talk with her father that now followed.

"I ain't against it in principle, pa.

Though I guess mother has a point over Uncle Rolf."

"That feckless fool," George Maledon grunted more amiably around his pipe. "Most all your ma's fambly were no-account one way or other. Tho' to hear her tell it you'd fancy 'em all pillows a the community." He began to spit, then recalled he was at home and swallowed it back instead.

His daughter gave a tolerant laugh, still regarding him closely with her set-together eyes that were like his own as to pale color.

"Personally, pa, I can't see how it was worth anyone bettin' on you to beat this other hangman. I mean, if that big city daily gave you the title that I — that mother mislikes so much, well, *of course* I don't know much about such things, but wouldn't it mean you're so bound to win that any such bets on you would be a sure-fire certainty, and so hardly worth placing?"

He looked at her with an amazed

gratified beam. "Well of course it would mean that goin' strictly on the facts, girly," he told her with an eloquent pipe jab. "Take my word, there ain't no contest as such in this *a-tall*! Was only them dumbos at the Grand Lodge as made my odds fade off so I'm a good bet now! They went an' timed me when I was only half-hurryin' on a standard job, then jumped to the notion that was my best shot! That's how come my odds tumbled down in the lodge book." He gave a reedy blustering laugh. "Take my word, any bucko who hooks on to them present odds is makin' a right smart investment."

Annie Maledon gave no sign of being swayed by that opinion. She was well aware that the Prince of Hangmen was not exactly impartial as to his own ability. All the same . . . she did tend to think that his title must mean he would win out over this other neck-stretcher. And if the present odds on him were as good as he said . . . But then she thought of another difficulty in the way of it.

Her small bosom heaved a sentimental sigh. "Well, I guess that's a piece of luck for the old soldiers, then, pa — and hardluck for all others who can't go to the lodge and take advantage of those odds. All those you call civilians."

"Like you say, you can't foller such things," her father said with fond indulgence. (The way he'd always liked to indulge her, long ago.) "But y'see, girly, the lodge book they done on me will sure as hell pull down the odds in all them other books they say are got up on it. Take them desk jumpers at the First National, for instance. They say there's a book going there. Now men a that stripe know doodly shit about hangin's — but they're fast minded about money moves. So I reckon they'll foller the lodge on it. Less'n I miss my guess, them other book setters will all foller the lodge, thinkin' that's where the hottest knowledge is at — goddam fools . . . "

Annie nodded, and gave him a more genuine smile than hitherto. It so happened she knew an old beau who worked at the First National. She had a vague feeling he had been promoted since then. She tried to recollect how sorely they had parted — but there were too many others in between.

However, she thought she might stop by at the bank in the morning, and maybe strike him for some independent financial advice.

★ ★ ★

Although the unexpected chat with his daughter left him with a feeling of faint unease, he didn't really believe that the fact a few women now knew of the record attempt would make things much riskier for him than they were before.

About a week later, early in the new month, he was in his workshop one evening fashioning a noose for the next day. Other lengths of cord were being stretched out on the pulley. It was getting colder now, and for the first time since last spring he'd lit his pot-bellied centre stove. He had the fire-box piled high with coal and cordwood, and it crackled companionably close by his toes; for he had kicked his boots off to enjoy renewing that old wintertime habit. The new windows where the old stable doors had been were starting to stream on the inside.

That was probably why the company took him by surprise. Usually anyone crossing the yard to the workshop could be spotted through those windows. But the first he knew of his visitors was when the four of them stepped in quietly by way of the half-doors entrance.

He looked up from filing the brass eye on the noose; then at once dropped the file and reached to the near drawer in his workbench. But then the one heading up the group — the more gentish one with the Chesterfield coat and a small black moustache ending in twisted needle-points — rapped out: "Hold it, Maledon!" And he took in the little hawkbilled and silver-mounted .38 in that one's hand.

His own dithered a second, then wandered reluctantly back to his lap. His gaze flicked quickly over the other three obvious hard buggers. One had a gun in a short home-made holster. Another had a pair of steel-bowed specs that were not in line with his pounded-looking eyes. The fourth one wore a worsted suit that looked nearly as ancient as his own emigrant-style article from Germany. He was heeled too, and had something else bulging on his other side which could have been a pocketful of brass knuckles.

"Somethin' as I can do for you gents?" he said hoarsely. He was wondering if those damnfool women had sent them over here, or if they'd found their own way across to him. He hoped strongly it was the first — for Eunice wasn't that much a fool she wouldn't be this minute flying downstreet for help, if they had called at the house.

The one with the slapped-back fedora and the needle-points shifted the angle of his deadly little weapon, so that its silver trim glinted in the lampshine from above. "That's sensible," he said pleasantly. "Since all we want is a little talk with you."

"About what, mister?" (Though he reckoned to know goddam what by now . . .)

"We're just off the train from Little Rock," Needle-points told him in a conversational way. "These gentlemen are my business associates."

"Yeh they look like business associates too," the hangman said wryly. "Let's get to it, mister. You've come here in some way to do with that numbskull contest a mine with Zeb Allen, ain't you . . . "

Needle-points beamed around sarcastically at his associates. "Appears this is not just a prince of his kind, gentlemen. This is a *modest and unassuming* prince . . . But perhaps his modesty is not exactly good news for us, huh?"

"No it ain't," the one in the hard worsted said tersely. (Those were a set of knuckles on him, he would swear.) Sweat beads began to pop out among his hair roots in a way that had little to do with the stove heat.

The one in worsted jerked his head at the big one in specs; the one who could have been an old booth fighter. "What d'you figure then, Clay?"

Clay shambled forward. He set a lumpy paw on the stable owner's shoulder, plucking him upright, while he adjusted his specs with the other one. "Try movin' around a bit, hangerman," he said in a broken-voiced husk that was of a piece with the rest of him.

George Maledon began to refuse that impertinent request. But it seemed inadvisable. Snarling in silence, he tried moving around a bit.

"Holy mother," Clay husked unflatteringly. He took a step closer and ripped out the tails of the executioner's hickory workshirt. Then his hands moved testingly over his exposed upper body.

"These pect'rals ain't too bad," he reported presently. "Pound for pound and considerin' he's an old Joe this age, I'd say he's useful up above. Down below is another story though."

"*Thanks a lot!*" the Prince of Hangmen exploded. "*I'm proud to know I've got you boys' approval!*"

"Clay didn't go that far," Needlepoints said with a finger wag and an oily smirk. "Get his pants down, Clay."

"NOW JUST YOU — !" But then the one in the worsted suit shook out the brass items he'd brought along, so that what small shred of doubt he had retained on that score melted away. His indignation seemed to do the same. But rather than have Clay's ungentle touch spray his flies over the

207

cobbles he unbuttoned and lowered his pants himself, displaying his longhandle underwear.

As he did so he focused Needlepoints with a flat glare. "You take this much farther on, son, and I'll have a tally to set straight with you," he told him softly.

The boss man merely chuckled. "Stay loose, Maledon. This isn't what you think now at all. I'm not some revenge-crazed relation come to level with you for one of your drops. This is strictly business — though I doubt it will be for much longer. Clay — don't peel that inner wool off him. By the tang of them from over here they've prob'ly been on him that long you'd take his skin off with them."

Clay was now kneading his way carefully and expertly up and down his shanks. And suddenly he grasped the meaning behind these indignities he was suffering. His snarl became more of a rictus than ever, though he kept to his helpless near-silence.

At last the ex-bruiser stood up from his examination. "It's like I pegged him when he first walked," he shrugged in open disgust. "He just ain't got nothin' *there*, Henry. Now, if I had him out on the roads for a good month, mebbe something could be made of him. But this thing is goin' down sooner, ain't that so?" His puffy eyes now bothered to meet George Maledon's for the first time since he had been concentrating on the rest of him.

"Iffen you're referencin' to my contest," he mumbled, with a pathetic try at aloofness, "it's been set for the twelfth."

Clay gave a hopeless whistle through a prominent gap in his teeth. Hard-worsted gravely shook his head. Home-made holster flipped his wad of cut plug out of his cheek and put it away in a pocket, with an air of keeping it for better and more rewarding days ahead. Needle-points emitted a long sigh of regret. Then he said briskly:

"Well then, seems that's it, boys.

Sorry about this, Maledon. No offence intended. But before I invested in you I felt I had to check out your condition. As you must know, you're bracing a much younger man. In my opinion — and I think I speak for my associates — your best chance would seem to lie in prayer. Right, we'll say goodnight and leave you to your work, then."

With a final smooth grin at the hangman's now apoplectic countenance, Needle-points touched his fedora and began to lead the four of them out of the workshop. But Clay hung back a little. And when his boss was still just short of the half-doors the old bruiser called out: "Wait on a bit, Henry . . . "

"I've just recalled something," he husked when Needle-points swung round again. "Did you ever hear tell of the humming dinger between Jimmy Raven and Oceola Johnson?"

"No I didn't — and is it relevant?" Needle-points grunted impatiently.

"Well it just might be," Clay continued, with another despising scowl back at George Maledon. "Johnson was going on sixty at the time, havin' tried to retire about ten years before. By then *he* had missin' muscles too, after the style of this ol' hanger. But he won that bout with Raven after but one day's training. And I know how it was done, cause Billy Armitage told me how when he was managin' me a space after that weird vict'ry happened. Billy had the managin' of Johnson then, y,see though ever'one said it was downright impossible to make a chairbound wreck with no legs stand up to a middling fighter in full training. But Billy had this theory it could be done. And what he did was he had Johnson dance till he dropped."

Home-made holster now made his first contribution to the talk. "Huh — this old coot ain't got no partner is what I'm thinkin'." He uttered a few mirthless hoots, then went back to gawping at the picture gallery.

211

"When I say dance I don't mean like really *dance*," Clay croaked on. "I mean Billy made him run on the spot. Till he sheerly dropped, downright unconscious, like I say."

All four now turned to re-inspect the quailing hangman. "What's your heart like, Maledon?" Needle-points enquired thoughtfully.

"Plumb bad! Plumb shaky, and allus was from birth!" he blurted out. But Clay shook his head in a knowing way that curdled his own blood.

"That's bullshit. I checked that out. There's a steady bong-bong goin' under those skinny old slats. Of course I can't guarantee you, Henry. But I'd reckon his top half is good enough to keep him alive through it. And if he did live — like I say, it's sheerly wonderful how that can puff up the muscles."

Needle-points had holstered his .38. He now tapped it reflectively for several minutes, then pulled it again. He pointed it at the executioner. "Run," he said simply.

212

"*Oh no!*" George Maledon told him in the shrill accents of one already tried past endurance. "You ain't about to dance *me* around like some pilgrim come out West! I'll see you in hell first!"

Needle-points pulled a face and checked his loads. "Boys — a little supporting fire-power if you please." He began to blast off shots, with unnerving accuracy, very near to George Maledon's stubbornly planted socked feet.

The others did not shoot so well. Their shots were scary in a different way. Bullets spanged off the stove, one screaming past his nose and ploughing into a sandbag on the end of one of the dangling ropes. Another ricochetted off the bench top and jangled out a window.

"*Hear that?*" he hollered hysterically. "*You boys had bestways fog it afore that fetches me some help from you crazy scuts!*"

. . . But by then he was running. He wasn't precisely aware of when he'd given in and started to, but now his feet were scissoring up and down in an involuntary manner that had seemed totally beyond them when he'd been working out with a skip rope.

The leisurely and sadistic fusillade continued — and still no one came . . . Where were those numbskulled women of his at? If they'd run down the road when this caper started, some law should be coming any second now . . .

. . . By God it would *need* to come soon. What with the stove heat, and this constant prancing on the painful cobbles, moisture was now pouring off of him like he was spot-running in Florida swampland instead of an Arkansas stable . . .

"Hold up you loco'd sumbitches!" he screeched above the explosions. *"I'm dyin', I'm dyin! — for gawsake hold up!"*

All that appeal from the heart (in every way) drew him a slug which clipped his ankle bone. His screams

214

soared higher, and his legs likewise. Despite the cauldron inside him that was now fast rising to boiling point he was still dimly aware of the one they called Clay, the ex-boxer, peering at him with a look of expert dispassion in between picking his shots.

Gunsmoke now drifted in a pall about the workshop, its acrid fumes blending with the iron tang from the hot stove. He pounded on, gasping and choking. *Where was their Godforsook law?* It just made no sense that Euny and the girl wouldn't have fetched some roaming field dep, or a city harness bull, to his aid by now . . .

But then came a memory that had enough power to send a chill through him, in spite of all his surging and raging heat. It was a memory from earlier that day at breakfast-time. A half-ignored memory of Eunice saying: "I'll be home late today, George. Mrs Wicks is holdin' a quilting party for showers for her Jane and I said I'd pitch in. I'll leave you yours in the oven, since Annie'll be out too with her latest one."

So he might as well forget all about help coming. This was set to end the way these white-skinned Kiowas meant it to, with him collapsed on these cobbles . . .

Final realization seemed to bring that ending suddenly closer, with a faltering and swaying of his senses. But still the merciless bullets came probing and goading, and still his numbed limbs sprinted insanely to nowhere. The walls and their daguerreotypes of the dead began to tilt at strange angles.

And then, with a gobbling cry, a hotter wave than ever rose suddenly into his head and he felt the commencement of his fall.

He wasn't totally out after that; there was a small core of consciousness still deeply buried in him. Their voices came to him via that core, without identity, as if from a distant planet.

"Yeh, well, I know what I think of that idea."

"I tell you it worked that time."

"It ain't worked this time. What it's got us down there is one unbackable dead hangman. Or good as."

"I ain't so sure. Oceola Johnson looked just the — "

"I've heard too much about Johnson. You plunge on this old feller by yourself if you want to. But the five thou stays kept back for Kentucky time. You know where you are in Kentucky."

"Listen to the man."

"He's right too. After this I'll stick to nags over hangmen every time."

"Well I grant it don't appear very likely he's going to win his contest now. I guess he was a mite old to be trainable."

"The hell you say. Let's get out of here."

12

AFTER that he knew he had to end it.

The decision didn't stem so much from the actual mistreatment he'd suffered. Apart from huge swellings in his calves and thighs, so that he could barely walk for several days, he seemed unaffected by his experience. He reckoned that the onetime pugilist had known something, when he'd opined that his heart would stand the strain.

But the sheer fact that news of his attempt had spread to a fourth class gaming syndicate based well outside Fort Smith was a sign he dared not ignore. If he didn't end it now, he would bring down total ruin on himself as sure as hell; and not to mention ruining his Grand Lodge pals, and likely a passel more reckless punters that he didn't even know of.

Because of his swollen limbs, he'd reported sick at the courthouse. If the judge now pulled ahead of him with their joint workload that was just too bad — he could hardly hang anyone if he couldn't climb his own gibbet steps. (And as for doing that in record time, the men from Little Rock had put paid to that stupid aim once and for all by making him a wreck; though he told himself that might be just as well, now it had gone sour in a more serious way.)

He had plenty of time to mull the situation over, while sitting and fretting at home all day. What needed doing was only too clear: how was another matter.

But slowly — and shockingly — the one possible answer sank into him. He would have to destroy the creation that had made him famous. He would have to burn down the hanging machine.

No other answer could guarantee the end of the contagion of betting fever that he'd set loose; without he was willing to give Zeb Allen best in public — which he still wasn't. That would be more than his spirit could bear. But if the great hanging machine was no more (and with maybe a face-saving rumor spread around town that Zeb had paid to have it done to keep his record), he could still duck out of this whole mess. Though at some cost.

Of course, there would need to be another gallows built in its place. There was a trace of solace for him in that reflection. Sometimes he had wondered idly about the challenge of operating a twenty-man-er. But he'd doubted that Parker would ever let him build one that big. He knew he didn't approve of excessiveness. Even so . . .

But he knew really that he was only trying to cheer up by harboring such idle thoughts; he knew really there would be nothing like that gallows of his seen ever again. The changing namby-pamby times were all against such feats of lethal invention.

Sitting alone one forenoon, in the shut-down and depressing atmosphere of his workshop, he reached a final decision. He would travel well out of town to buy the raft of coal oil he'd need, so that no one could finger him for it afterward. He would do that right now, before he could weaken. And come Saturday night he would kill his own death machine.

★ ★ ★

But when the next Saturday night came, things didn't go off quite as planned.

It was a night black as pitch — ideal for his purpose. Raucous gangs of drunks were rampaging unchecked around town over on Cocaine Hill and the Choctaw Strip — also ideal, in that they could plausibly be blamed for starting the conflagration. Though in fact nobody else had strayed into the area of the old fort buildings but himself.

He managed to make himself douse the four huge corner balks, clear to platform height. And he managed to make himself haul several more full cans up above, and soak the three traps and the lower parts of the thick trunk of cross-beam. Then, after he came down the steps for the last time, dousing each one in turn, he stood for a longish space in the gallows yard while he felt more like an executioner than he ever had before. But finally he made himself strike a sulphur match.

In the next short period of time, while the match burned down to his fingers, George Maledon learned that the only possible solution was one that he could not make himself apply.

★ ★ ★

J. Warren Reed entered the lobby of the LeFlore Hotel, glancing at a chalk-and-slate notice board that was stood off to one side of the carpet strip on a tripod stand. The printed chalk letters read: *9PM. CRYSTAL ROOM. BAR SUPPER.*

The dapper attorney sighed to himself as he removed his gloves and topcoat, displaying an immaculate dark suit of hairy Scottish wool. Folding the coat over his arm, and holding the gloves and an ivory-handled cane, he went in search of Vernon Petty, the hotel's proprietor.

He found him in the Crystal Room itself, directing a team of waitresses who were putting final touches to the pair of long tables, resplendent with starched linen and the establishment's best cutlery service. Overhead, four sizable chandeliers that the Petty family had shipped in from Illinois were glittering attractively.

Warren Reed, in his self-assured way, tapped the hotelman's shoulder with his cane. "Ah, Petty, a word in your ear . . . The guide notice you've put up is somewhat misleading. Rather than *Bar Supper* I would suggest *Bar Association Dinner*."

"Sure thing, Mr Reed," Petty gushed and fawned. "I'll see to it d'rectly, sir."

In fact Vernon Petty was a staunch pro-hanger who had very little time for the famous defense lawyer. But he knew quality when he saw it, and pegged this tall West Virginian as one who had it in spades. He moved forward to take his coat and extras; but not before Reed had tossed them carelessly into his arms.

When the proprietor had gone away, Reed bestowed an all-round smile upon the busy waitresses. He stroked his dark walrus mustache and wandered casually up and down the tables, looking for his own place card.

When he found it, he picked it up and glanced toward the head of that table, where Judge Parker would presently be seated. Taking the card, he sauntered to the place that had been set immediately to the right of the table head. The card there read: Mrs Wilfred Arbuthnot. He moved on around until he was scrutinizing the card on the opposite side of the board: Mr James Douglas.

With another bland grin at a nearby bustling girl, the lawyer switched his card with that of Mr James Douglas. Under the waitress's scandalized — but uncertain — gaze, he took Mr Douglas's card to where his own had lately been. And then he ambled out of the room in search of a whisky.

★ ★ ★

"I assure you, madam, that is my own settled view as well as yours," the judge was saying kindly to Mrs Arbuthnot. "In these lax times, so-called insanity is a familiar plea which should always be treated with marked circumspection — nay, I would go farther than that and even say with *suspicion*. But come, these are hardly topics suited to a handsome lady on a social occasion," he went on gallantly. One of his huge hands tugged at a choking collar stud.

Mrs Arbuthnot bridled and subsided, grateful that her duty exchange with her formidable dinner partner was now over. J. Warren Reed saw his chance. His eyes took on a wicked glint.

"How expensive these affairs are becoming, Judge! At this rate I'm not at all sure that Viola and I will be able to afford the next one." He gave a light laugh. "But perhaps you are seeking to defray the cost yourself by the same hopeful means that I understand many of our friends here tonight have resorted to."

The judge frowned. It had been a disagreeable surprise that Petty had put him next to his unprincipled courtroom adversary. He had already shared the few basic civilities with him that he had deemed incumbent. Now he said frostily:

"Defray the cost, sir? I am afraid that I don't follow you."

Warren Reed's face wore a smile of cruel satisfaction; though he had been almost sure he hadn't known. He relished his next words.

"Sorry, Judge, I'll explain. I'm referring to the contest between Maledon and the other well-known hangman fellow, what's his name, Adams? Apparently it is to decide which of them can despatch a victim in the shortest possible time. Hardly in the best possible taste, don't you agree? But there are wagers on the result being laid all over the city and beyond — indeed, as I implied, there is a book going on amongst members of this venerable body gathered here now," he finished gleefully.

Parker's already florid complexion had become distinctly more so. He set down his spoon with a clatter, Petty's excellent cherry cobbler now quite forgotten. "*Book?*" he repeated blankly. "How, pray, can a book *go on*? One *reads* books."

"Not this kind," Reed assured him with trembling lips. (How he would make Vi chortle over this scene when they got home . . .) "The word also has a betting connotation. I believe that most favorable odds can now be obtained on Maledon, since it is said that his health has failed lately."

Judge Parker eyed his informant with near-hatred, sensing the malice that lay behind these polite disclosures. Surging wrathfully to his feet, he tugged the bib from his glossy shirt front and threw it violently aside. Then he lumbered out of the room, deaf to the murmur of talk behind him which that abrupt exit had provoked.

★ ★ ★

About an hour later, he emerged in much the same state from his executioner's dooryard, slamming its gate violently behind him. Then he fiercely strode the two blocks of North Thirteenth street that separated their two abodes, muttering the while beneath his breath.

Mary Parker was in their bedroom when he went looking for her, to inform her of the outrage he had discovered. She was sorting through several of her dresses, laid out on both their beds. She glanced up from them vaguely.

"Ah, Isaac . . . I trust I was not missed unduly at the dinner — did you enjoy it?"

"Scarcely!" he burst out. "You will not credit this, I am sure, but Maledon has become involved in *wagers upon the speed of an execution*! That fellow Reed told me at the hotel — exulting in it, I might add! Of course, as soon as I heard I straightaway left the LeFlore and went to confront Maledon! I spoke to him with all the severity I could summon up, as you may imagine! — and do you know all he could plea in his defence? — *this*! 'It may seem like nonsense to you, sir, but Zeb Allen and me see it different like'.

"Those were his very words! Have you ever heard the like, Mary? When I *think how many times* I have impressed upon him the *essential gravity* of his task, and the importance of giving not the *slightest excuse* to those fools in the Capital to reduce our powers even more than they already have! *And now this*! Well, he will have to quit his position! I have already made that abundantly clear to him! The claims of our long association are *as nothing* compared to the enormity of what he has done!"

Mary raised a soft white hand to her throbbing temples. "Dearest — if you could shout a little less . . . and as for Maledon, well I cannot pretend to be very surprised. He has erred so grievously in his main — his main purpose in life, that if he is now erring in other ways besides that is only to be — "

"*Erring?*" he cut in explosively. "Ahem. I am sorry, my dear . . . But I have really been very provoked by him on this occasion. It is really very shocking indeed."

"Well I daresay it is," Mary replied with a touch of asperity that was most unusual from her (if he had not been too distracted to notice it). "But so is something else, Isaac. I have been invited to my niece's wedding in Boston. That is to say, to young Maeve's wedding." She paused, and met his eyes with a speaking look in her own.

Still locked in his fury over the wagers, and the travesty of justice allied to them, he did not at first grasp her full import. But then he did; and he grasped the dire meaning of all those sad old dresses spread on the beds.

"Ah. Maeve, yes . . . " he said heavily. "She is from your New England side, is she not?"

As a young Missouri lawyer — and despite his good prospects of becoming much more than that — he had suffered no small humiliation as a suitor, at the hands of the highly Catholic O'Tooles. And even when he had become a Congressman they had still made him feel, whenever possible, that Mary had thrown herself away on a Methodist. He was now grimly anticipating what she was about to tell him.

"Isaac, I just *cannot* appear in Boston wearing any of these old things! Indeed, I shall require a whole new outfit for such a grand occasion as this is bound to be. I know that this invitation is badly timed, indeed it is . . . but I can hardly not go, now can I? It would be taken very remiss by my aunt and the rest of them. No, I must go — it is incumbent," she finished in a voice of financial doom.

He made a feeble effort to avoid his fate. "Speaking for myself, Mary, I have always bethought me how very handsome that — er — one in the middle is. That nice dun-colored one."

"Yes, but dearest, only *look* at the poor old basque that goes with it," she said hopelessly. Then her tone grew determined again. "I am very sorry, Isaac — but sizable funds will have to be found for this visit."

"But we have no such funds," he

declared on a note of rising desperation. Never until this moment had he so felt the ludicrous parsimony of his federal salary. "*What is not there* can hardly be surrendered, my dear."

"You could always see Pettigrew at the bank again," she persisted resolutely.

"No, I think not — not after that last emergency of James's," he ruled firmly. He winced as he recalled the banker's unrespectful comments on that occasion. He had needed all his authority to make the man oblige him. "There is just no way of doing it," he told her sadly.

But by then Temptation was already beginning to unfold its dark wings in his mind.

* * *

Most of that night he lay awake, manfully wrestling with it. It was so *sheerly appalling* to a man of his convictions. To even contemplate it, after the way he had just been lecturing Maledon, made him a total hypocrite — a creature of straw . . .

And besides that, to be strictly practical — surely it was an absurd risk to take? Things were hard enough for them already, heavens knew, without the risk of losing the little they had put by for the future.

. . . But wait a minute: hadn't that dreadful fellow Reed said something reassuring on that head? Something about Maledon's health making him a better . . . prospect? But there again, there must be two sides to that . . .

Staring up sightlessly at the black ceiling, he tried to remember how well his henchman had been looking when he left him; but that was hard to establish in the then circumstances . . . His state of sin had taken marked precedence over that of his health, so far as he was concerned at the time . . .

Eventually he fell into a light doze; where his various preposterous thoughts and doubts continued to torment him just below the surface.

★ ★ ★

George Maledon was braced for the summons to wait directly on the Old Man, when he received it from the court caller as the two of them met in the porch early next day.

A few moments later he was haggardly facing his equally haggard-looking employer; and then Isaac Parker said quietly and surprisingly: "Good morning, Mr Maledon. Before we speak of other concerns, I wish to enquire how matters are . . . set in train regarding this fellow Higgs."

The hangman blinked. He'd been all ready to be officially fired — yet here they were running a total different track, it seemed. But then he guessed despondingly that the Old Man just wanted to be brought up to date all round before he fired him. He gave an indifferent shrug.

"That's all taken care of. I can put the run on that clerk any time you choose — or show you how to, iffen I ain't here to do it," he finished with a bitter press of his lips.

"You are quite sure of that?"

"Sure I'm sure."

"I am very glad to hear it. That is a great weight off my mind. I think, perhaps, I do not wish to hear the precise details of how it has been achieved — but I am very much obliged to you. Indeed, upon due reflection, I feel this, er, private service to the court greatly mitigates the other matter we spoke of last night. Therefore I have decided that your, ahem, contest should be allowed to proceed as planned. I would only insist that the condemned men who take part in it should be willing volunteers, and fully appraised of the nature of . . . what is intended. If such volunteers cannot be found, then I shall have to withdraw this consent."

He had been determined to include that small sop to his conscience; and highly pathetic it now seemed. This must be the most shameful conversation of his entire life, he realized dully.

An astounded grin was now spreading across George Maledon's wan face.

"That won't be no problem! Why, those boys on Death Row would all be proud to be in the three as gets chosen for my contest! They've got a book goin' on that too up there, to make up a double!" He paused, looking at Parker, then went on more tactfully: "Are you sure you mean this, Y'r Honor? I swear to God you won't regret it!"

The judge winced again, as though he had been struck. He did not desire the name of the Almighty to be invoked in these — of all — proceedings. He said in a slightly choked tone: "There is another condition that I should stress to you. I wish the minimum of witne — that is to say, of bystanders to be present on this unusual occasion."

"That wish jumps together with mine, sir. I only want a couple of local reporters to be there just for the record. Heh-heh! Yeh, just for the record like. Elsewise, that Zeb Allen will try and say it was rigged somehow."

Judge Parker touched a hand to his forehead, his elbow pressing heavily on the desk. He told himself there was still time to turn back; but knew that he would not, unless perhaps . . .

"Tell me, is your health good at present? It has seemed to me of late that you have looked a trifle pale at times."

He peered intently; and George Maledon wondered what that look minded him of. At first he couldn't peg it. Then it came to him that (however weirdly) it made him think of the way those hardcases from Little Rock had inspected him, just before they started to shooting.

He pushed that weird comparing impatiently out of his head. "I'm fine, sir. I wasn't so chipper backalong, but I've come back real strong."

He was telling the plain truth there.

That ex-slugger in the betting syndicate must have known something about muscles, as he'd claimed. For ever since the stiffness had gone off he had felt like a young colt in the legs department. He hadn't the least shred of doubt now that he would beat Zeb to flinders when the time came.

Isaac Parker nodded, making the ultimate fateful decision. He had turned faintly grey about the face. But his head remained cool.

"Proceed, if you will, with getting rid of Higgs. We do not want him still here when he might try to stir up trouble over this . . . contest."

"Will do, Your Honor. I'll handle that. That one's goose is as good as cooked, take my word."

"Splendid . . . oh, before you go, do you happen to know if Deputy Anstey is still in the city? I suppose Colonel Hall may have sent him out on assignment again by now, but I wanted to see him to — to commend him for his last tour of duty."

Maledon's brightened up visage now wore a slight frown. He was nearly sure that Heck Anstey had mentioned to him that he'd already seen Parker about his last trip in the Territory. But maybe he had misunderstood him. Right now he was too taken up with his own affairs to care either way.

"I guess he's apt to be still around, sir. Saw him in a bull session by the marshal's office only a couple of days back. Shall I send him up here if I see him again?"

"If you would be so kind, Maledon. And — and thank you . . . "

★ ★ ★

After he had left the Old Man he took a short stroll in prominent spots about the town. He limped pretty badly on that stroll, and sometimes stopped to catch his breath.

In actual fact he felt on top of the world after the fine news. But now the contest was on again it made obvious sense to copper things all he could ahead of his own considerable bet on himself. He'd already planned to use the Chamber of Commerce for that purpose, for he reckoned there would be no lay-off problem in that class, and less chance of some bugger hieing off with the pot.

Once he felt he had been seen enough he turned his shuffling steps toward home. There, he took a large unsealed envelope from his workbench drawer. Then he went downtown again to see the court clerk.

★ ★ ★

"Ah, Maledon, come right in!" Crawford Higgs sang out brightly when he saw who it was by his door. "I've been expecting you . . . do pray be seated."

He did so, looking cagily at that oily phiz with the stretched grin pinned firmly back in place again. Yep: this was a skunk who figured himself shed of the baitpan trap . . .

"I've got a piece of news for *you*, Mister Clerk," he told him evenly. "Won't need for you to take that trip to Saint Lou now, since my plans have changed some."

"Is that a fact?" the clerk purred back. "Not that it matters, because I wouldn't have gone anyway. I've got news for you, Maledon. My wife has pulled out and left me. I take it you can work out for yourself where that leaves you, my friend," he said with huge sarcasm.

"I know where it leaves me," he agreed mildly. He looked out the window and yawned.

Crawford Higgs frowned. "Maybe you're too stupid to see what I mean — so I'll spell it out. Now my wife's gone you can't go running to her about my night on First Street. And since you're tied in yourself to that killing it led to, you can't hold that over me either. You've got nothing on me at all now. So what I say to you my friend is — "

"Afore you get unpolite you'd ought to scan these." He tossed the envelope contemptuously on the desk.

The look of triumph melted away pretty damned quick off those unpleasant features once Higgs had taken a peek at the thin set of daguerreotypes inside. "*Where — ? How — ? Oh my God . . .* "

"I'll say you take a good pitcher, Mister Clerk," he allowed harshly. "Not that I'd pin them ones up along of my own collection. They wouldn't blend in so well. Now, what was we sayin' afore we strayed off the point?"

Higgs finally dragged his eyes from the photo shots and fixed them like hooded hot lamps on his visitor. "You had a picturemaker in the next room . . . "

"That's right, sonny — I had me a picturemaker in the next room, to get the first part of the action through a wall hole." He gave a dour reedy chuckle. "The second part nigh kilt him with fright, if that's any interest to you. I guess it's an odd word to use on you, but there's a moral in this boghole you've blundered into: *when you're steady custom at a sportinghouse make sure you stick to unsteady hours.*" He hawked on the floor and gave a sagacious nod.

"What do you aim to do now?" Higgs mumbled savagely. He half-tore the photos across, then quit that futile gesture and began to sob.

"Depends on you. You set there an' pen a nice letter to the judge offerin' him your resernation, I can prob'ly fix to see you get his testimony so's you can land another clerk job — like in a store," he added with emphasis. "Or iffen you want it handled the other way, I can get my pal Hal Rathbone to pull off some more a those and they get sent to Washin'ton for studying on."

He waited placidly while the court clerk killed him with those wet hopeless eyes. Then Crawford Higgs slowly reached the pen from the inkstand.

Colonel Henry Harvard-Hall, the U.S. marshal based at Fort Smith, had few illusions about the body of men he was nowadays in charge of.

Many of them had been on the dodge themselves before joining the force. Others had left it in order to go on the dodge. And of the ones at any time presently employed, several would be forever thinking about going on the dodge. That situation was partly due to their lousy pay — but also, in the old brasshat's private opinion, because they were on the whole a pretty lousy and sloppy bunch of men besides.

So once he had learned that his deputies were running a book on the court hangman, he had moved swiftly to get things put on a proper footing; otherwise, he knew that whoever drew the job of running the book would in all likelihood run off *with* the book, shortly before the contest took place.

It wasn't that he felt his own figuring

ability exceeded theirs; far from it. He had sat in sometimes on complicated gaming amongst his largely unlettered force that would have baffled some of the sharpest minds of his own grad year at the Point. No: it was just their innate dishonesty that had made him take over the bets on their behalf.

He was drinking a cup of coffee in his office when someone knocked on the door. He licked the brown edging of his short white mustache and barked: "Enter!"

"Mornin', sir, Colonel."

"Oh, it's you, Heck . . . what can I do for you? Beginning to ache again for the field, huh? Well, it won't be long now before I — "

"No, it ain't that, sir. Got another bet for you to stick on George for me."

The marshal inclined his smooth white head. "Sure — but I hope you know what you're doing, man. Maledon has gone down a lot since this time yesterday. I can let you have him now at four for eleven — but I warn you they say he's in shocking shape. Still, it's your funeral. Let's have it, then."

A moment later his bright blue eyes were goggling at the bunches of banded bills on his table. Then they narrowed and peered up shrewdly at the deputy. "Where did you come by a sum like this, Anstey? It somewhat exceeds your first stake," he observed dryly.

Heck Anstey's battered hound-dog face stayed impassive. "Life savin's, Colonel. I've got this certain feelin' in my bones about George. I mean to say, he's Prince of Hangmen, ain't he . . . The way I see it this will set me up in my retirement."

"Or else send you begging through the streets. However, that's your concern — so long as you've come by it honestly. I advise you against such recklessness but . . . God damn it, Heck, this will mean I'll have to get on to the people at First National. I can't carry anything like this much on our ledger," he said crossly. "Oh well, leave it to me. Once I get this counted you can have your slip."

Heck Anstey wore a faint grin on his leathery chops when he left the office. He still couldn't quite believe what he'd been asked to arrange. For a wistful moment he tried to figure what a win on that layout *would* do for his retirement. It would be worth lighting a shuck with, that was for sure.

But the long-serving deputy didn't seriously ponder that course of action. He knew how far Parker's arm could reach. No, if that crock of gold should come up, he would settle for what he had been promised for his service and silence.

★ ★ ★

As soon as he took his familiar stance at the corner window, he saw that one of his conditions for allowing the spectacle had predictably come to naught — for the square below was as full of unregenerate humanity as he had ever seen it.

He registered vaguely that other things were not as they should be: above all, the peculiarly different excitement of this crowd, which came to him despite the thick glass between him and them; their waves of hectic laughter, which even the most depraved of previous crowds had never sullied his ears with; the broadly smiling lines of deputies, struggling with uncommon tolerance to hold the people back from the gallows yard, themselves plainly infected by the general air of irreverence; and, of course, the still more extraordinary demeanour of the three doomed figures on the platform, chatting and chuckling together, although the deputy stood behind each had already performed Maledon's usual task of strapping their legs.

But all that was much as he had expected, and resigned himself to. What he was profoundly *unprepared* for was the weight of craven self-concern that was now overwhelming him.

. . . He must have been mad — quite mad. The next few minutes would assuredly see his total ruin . . . poor dear Mary, who deluded herself that her worst fate was to be denied a grand wedding . . . too soon would she discover what real poverty meant . . . and how those damnable O'Tooles would revel in his downfall! — to say nothing of the astonished delight of his foes in the Capital . . . *mad, quite, quite mad* . . .

A sudden raucous cheer swelled outside. His stricken eyes focused downward again. Maledon was now coming out from the jail basement, passing swiftly through the narrow passage that the deputies had kept open for him between the pressing ranks on each side. The cheers and laughter was now a continual roar, buffeting off the glass.

. . . What on Earth was Hall doing down there by the gibbet? The marshal had a pistol in his hand. He was gesturing with it at Maledon, requiring him to assume an odd crouched position at the foot of the steps. And then he was stiffly holding the gun over his own head, aiming it at the sky.

He realized belatedly what was about to happen, and grabbed hold of the once expensive Waltham timepiece that was chained to his waistcoat. He just had time to snap down its second-button as the report cracked out from below.

On the very edge of his vision he saw a familiar figure, leaping up the black steps. And in the same peripheral way he saw inverted sacks dropping down over the three heads, almost as one, after the Prince of Hangmen had gained platform height. He heard the familiar clatter of the trap, and caught the blur of downward movement so that his thumb snapped again on his watch button, almost involuntarily, as the three ropes tautened.

But really, throughout the whole of

those few seconds, his eyes had been held and hypnotized by the creeping and boding hand of his watch. And yet at first he just could not see what it now read! The extremity of his mental anguish had somehow made him blind!

But then he finally did see it. And, as on former occasions at this time and place, Isaac Parker once again sank to his knees in fervent communion with his Maker.

But of course there was an essential difference. This time, he was not praying for the victims of those who now swung gently to and fro beneath his vantage point. He was giving thanks for himself.

★ ★ ★

"Congratulations, pa! I knew you could! I just *knew*!"

George Maledon pushed his sparkling-eyed daughter gruffly away from their clinch, settling back in his easy chair with a wet glint in his own eyes. Of course he'd always known she still felt for him, despite her grown-up missish ways. But it was nice to have it shown now and then. He murmured: "Thanks, girly — but we don't wanna upset your ma, do we? You know her rule — no hangin' talk in the house limits."

Eunice Maledon caught the end of that remark from the kitchen. She stuck her curler-ragged head around the door, managing a dour smile.

"Well I guess you can do *just this once*, George — just as long as it don't become a habit."

He grunted and grinned, drawing hard on his fresh pipe load. He reckoned what he had achieved today didn't need much bragging up. It was the kind of thing which would get spoken of from here on, whenever high grade hangmen came together to chew the fat.

Yep . . . and even your average ignorant folks in the square today would be able to tell their kiddies and gran kiddies how they'd actual been there when the Prince of them all showed Zeb Allen where to head in — three times over, and with two clear seconds in hand.

THE END

Other titles in the
Linford Western Library:

TOP HAND
Wade Everett

The Broken T was big. But no ranch is big enough to let a man hide from himself.

GUN WOLVES OF LOBO BASIN
Lee Floren

The Feud was a blood debt. When Smoke Talbot found the outlaws who gunned down his folks he aimed to nail their hide to the barn door.

SHOTGUN SHARKEY
Marshall Grover

The westbound coach carrying the indomitable Larry and Stretch headed for a shooting showdown.

FARGO: PANAMA GOLD
John Benteen

With foreign money behind him, Buckner was going to destroy the Panama Canal before it could be completed. Fargo's job was to stop Buckner.

FARGO:
THE SHARPSHOOTERS
John Benteen

The Canfield clan, thirty strong were raising hell in Texas. Fargo was tough enough to hold his own against the whole clan.

PISTOL LAW
Paul Evan Lehman

Lance Jones came back to Mustang for just one thing — revenge! Revenge on the people who had him thrown in jail.

FARGO: MASSACRE RIVER
John Benteen

The ambushers up ahead had now blocked the road. Fargo's convoy was a jumble, a perfect target for the insurgents' weapons!

SUNDANCE: DEATH IN THE LAVA
John Benteen

The Modoc's captured the wagon train and its cargo of gold. But now the halfbreed they called Sundance was going after it . . .

HARSH RECKONING
Phil Ketchum

Five years of keeping himself alive in a brutal prison had made Brand tough and careless about who he gunned down . . .

GUNSLINGER'S RANGE
Jackson Cole

Three escaped convicts are out for revenge. They won't rest until they put a bullet through the head of the dirty snake who locked them behind bars.

RUSTLER'S TRAIL
Lee Floren

Jim Carlin knew he would have to stand up and fight because he had staked his claim right in the middle of Big Ike Outland's best grass.

THE TRUTH ABOUT SNAKE RIDGE
Marshall Grover

The troubleshooters came to San Cristobal to help the needy. For Larry and Stretch the turmoil began with a brawl and then an ambush.

WOLF DOG RANGE
Lee Floren

Will Ardery would stop at nothing, unless something stopped him first — like a bullet from Pete Manly's gun.

DEVIL'S DINERO
Marshall Grover

Plagued by remorse, a rich old reprobate hired the Texas Troubleshooters to deliver a fortune in greenbacks to each of his victims.

GUNS OF FURY
Ernest Haycox

Dane Starr, alias Dan Smith, wanted to close the door on his past and hang up his guns, but people wouldn't let him.

DONOVAN
Elmer Kelton

Donovan was supposed to be dead. Uncle Joe Vickers had fired off both barrels of a shotgun into the vicious outlaw's face as he was escaping from jail. Now Uncle Joe had been shot — in just the same way.

CODE OF THE GUN
Gordon D. Shirreffs

MacLean came riding home, with saddle tramp written all over him, but sewn in his shirt-lining was an Arizona Ranger's star.

GAMBLER'S GUN LUCK
Brett Austen

Gamblers seldom live long. Parker was a hell of a gambler. It was his life — or his death . . .

McALLISTER ON THE COMANCHE CROSSING
Matt Chisholm

The Comanche, McAllister owes them a life — and the trail is soaked with the blood of the men who had tried to outrun them before.

QUICK-TRIGGER COUNTRY
Clem Colt

Turkey Red hooked up with Curly Bill Graham's outlaw crew. But wholesale murder was out of Turk's line, so when range war flared he bucked the whole border gang alone . . .

CAMPAIGNING
Jim Miller

Ambushed on the Santa Fe trail, Sean Callahan is saved by two Indian strangers. But there'll be more lead and arrows flying before the band join Kit Carson against the Comanches.

SUNDANCE: SILENT ENEMY
John Benteen

A lone crazed Cheyenne was on a personal war path. They needed to pit one man against one crazed Indian. That man was Sundance.

LASSITER
Jack Slade

Lassiter wasn't the kind of man to listen to reason. Cross him once and he'll hold a grudge for years to come — if he let you live that long.

LAST STAGE TO GOMORRAH
Barry Cord

Jeff Carter, tough ex-riverboat gambler, now had himself a horse ranch that kept him free from gunfights and card games. Until Sturvesant of Wells Fargo showed up.

BRETT RANDALL, GAMBLER
E. B. Mann

Larry Day had the choice of running away from the law or of assuming a dead man's place. No matter what he decided he was bound to end up dead.

THE GUNSHARP
William R. Cox

The Eggerleys weren't very smart. They trained their sights on Will Carney and Arizona's biggest blood bath began.

THE DEPUTY OF SAN RIANO
Lawrence A. Keating and
Al. P. Nelson

When a man fell dead from his horse, Ed Grant was spotted riding away from the scene. The deputy sheriff rode out after him and came up against everything from gunfire to dynamite.

ARIZONA DRIFTERS
W. C. Tuttle

When drifting Dutton and Lonnie Steelman decide to become partners they find that they have a common enemy in the formidable Thurston brothers.

TOMBSTONE
Matt Braun

Wells Fargo paid Luke Starbuck to outgun the silver-thieving stagecoach gang at Tombstone. Before long Luke can see the only thing bearing fruit in this eldorado will be the gallows tree.

HIGH BORDER RIDERS
Lee Floren

Buckshot McKee and Tortilla Joe cut the trail of a border tough who was running Mexican beef into Texas. They stopped the smuggler in his tracks.

FIGHTING RAMROD
Charles N. Heckelmann

Most men would have cut their losses, but Frazer counted the bullets in his guns and said he'd soak the range in blood before he'd give up another inch of what was his.

LONE GUN
Eric Allen

Smoke Blackbird had been away too long. The Lequires had seized the Blackbird farm, forcing the Indians and settlers off, and no one seemed willing to fight! He had to fight alone.

THE THIRD RIDER
Barry Cord

Mel Rawlins wasn't going to let anything stand in his way. His father was murdered, his two brothers gone. Now Mel rode for vengeance.

HELL RIDERS
Steve Mensing

Wade Walker's kid brother, Duane, was locked up in the Silver City jail facing a rope at dawn. Wade was a ruthless outlaw, but he was smart, and he had vowed to have his brother out of jail before morning!

DESERT OF THE DAMNED
Nelson Nye

The law was after him for the murder of a marshal — a murder he didn't commit. Breen was after him for revenge — and Breen wouldn't stop at anything . . . blackmail, a frameup . . . or murder.

DAY OF THE COMANCHEROS
Steven C. Lawrence

Their very name struck terror into men's hearts — the Comancheros, a savage army of cutthroats who swept across Texas, leaving behind a bloodstained trail of robbery and murder.